LOVE IS A STORM

Love is a Storm

Debut novel
"Love on Shore"

ASHLYNN JOHNSON

For more titles and information, please visit: ajohnsonpublishing.com

Contents

Credits

ISBN: 978-1-0878-9795-0

Photo Credit goes to **Michelle Lawson Photography**. Thank you for your beautiful addition to my love story. Also, a huge thank you to Jennah and Steven for a wonderful picture.

About the Author

Ashlynn Johnson fell in love with writing fiction stories that pull her readers into books filled with romance, courage, and determination. She has a passion for helping others and using her talents to write incredible love stories that are not only relatable but true since portions of the story reflect real-life experiences. Ashlynn graduated from the University of Southern Indiana with both a Bachelor's and Master's Degree. She contributes to many local organizations within her community and makes every effort to ensure her readers feel every emotion she puts into her writing.

Ashlynn Johnson

Dedication

To my husband who has done nothing but love and support me from the beginning of our very own love story – I love you.

To all those who look for love; find happiness first and the rest will follow.

Lastly, to my two supportive sister-in-laws, thank you so much for your time, effort, and editorial skills. You helped make this book perfect!

Prologue

Life works in mysterious ways sometimes. Things tend to happen when you least expect them. In fact, sometimes things happen that you are not expecting at all. Courage and devotion are two things that can make or break one's life and love. Growing up, we are told that things happen for a reason. Also, we are told that if we work hard, good things will happen. Well, is that really the case? What if we work hard and that good thing never finds us? What if we chase it, and it never stops? Understanding life is how we grow and growing is the mystery behind it all.

Love is a Storm

Chapter 1

"Finals are just around the corner and I want all of you to be prepared," Shelby lectures. "I will be staying after school three days next week to help anyone who is having trouble with the last assignment. Please let me know if you need any help. I would be happy to stay late to work with you." Shelby trails off as the sound of the bell rang out at the end of the day. Watching all the kids close their books and dismiss, Shelby walks back to her desk to sit down. Looking around the room, she sighs and closes her eyes. Three more weeks she tells herself, just three more weeks.

It has been eight months since Shelby left Orange Beach. Eight months since her life changed forever. Caught up in Callie's life last summer, she never truly realized how much she was going to miss her best friend. That was until she realized she was not able to just stop by her apartment or meet Callie for a run anymore. Of course, she was happy for Nate and Callie, but even more thankful that Paul had gotten years in prison for his wrongdoings. She had not thought much about what her life would look like with the void of her best friend. Callie called Shelby almost every day. She would even FaceTime Shelby to show off the progress made on their house. The true void, however, was Shelby's secret. A secret, not even Callie had known. Shelby had tried to remove that summer from her mind. Too many things happened that she could never take back or change.

"I can't wait for you to see the house! We almost have it finished," Callie says through the phone. "Nate has been working so hard on getting the bedrooms done so I can start decorating. I was hoping it would be done by the time the wedding was here so you could stay with us, but Nate says it will still be a few more weeks until it's finished. Something about the plumbing and updating some electrical box thing...I don't know. I told him that probably wasn't a reason we couldn't stay there." Laughing to herself, Shelby replies, "Or it is a huge reason! Callie, if there is no plumbing and electric, how would we stay there at all?" Callie, pausing on the other line, says, "It would be like camping. You know, like when we used to camp outside at your parents' house. We didn't have electric or running water." Laughing even harder now, Shelby says, "Yeah, we didn't, but we did have that big thing people actually live in 20 feet away. A place called a house!"

Callie remarks, "I just wanted you to stay with us, I miss you so much!" "I know," Shelby says. "But, Ruby called and said she had a condo I could stay in for free for the weekend. Plus, do you think I want to sleep right next to you and Nate? No thanks!" She says with a chuckle. Callie laughs, "Not like you haven't before." "Don't remind me," Shelby groans. "Well, I can't wait until you get here," Callie exclaims. "Nate and I will be picking you up at the airport, so call if there are any changes with your flight." Shelby replies, "See you soon Callie, and hey, I miss you a ton, too."

Sophie and Max were finally tying the knot this weekend. Sophie had been planning the wedding for what seemed like a decade. Renovations at their boutique led them to postpone their wedding several times. Finally, they decided to put everything else on hold and focus on their love for one another. They set the date and stuck with it. Sophie asked Callie and Shelby to be bridesmaids, which both ladies graciously accepted.

Shelby was eager to get back to the beach, even if it was only for a weekend. She would be leaving on Sunday to return for her last few weeks of school, but what she had not told Callie was that she was coming back for the entire summer. Ruby reserved Shelby a condo for the whole summer. Everyone agreed to make it a surprise for Callie, knowing she would be so thrilled. Nate joked with Shelby when they spoke last week, "You know I'm going to get the boot for the summer, and you will be all she's worried about." Shelby teased him, "Nate, I'm all she's ever really been worried about. She just uses you for the extra bonus."

Nate just laughed and agreed she was probably right. Shelby knew deep down that this was not true, but loved teasing Nate any chance she got. Callie and Nate were deeply in love with each other, and Shelby was happy for them both, although sometimes a little jealous of what they had. Shelby thought she had found that, too, many years ago. She dated a guy for a little over a year, and when she poured her heart out to him, he simply told her he didn't feel the same way and ended their relationship. Two weeks later, she found out that he was engaged to another woman. Shelby's heart was completely broken, but being the strong woman she is she tried not to show how badly he hurt her. Deep down, she was humiliated and crushed. She dated guys before, but never anyone she really felt connected with. That is, until Liam. Until he walked into her world unexpectantly and she gave in too fast. He shattered her thoughts of a new beginning. Shaking her head thinking about him, muttering to herself. No Shelby, remove him from your mind. He's not worth your time. You are a strong, independent woman who deserves better. Smiling, she took a deep breath and decided to finish packing for the summer.

Jumping and screaming, the two best friends run towards each other, Nate trailing behind Callie. Shelby lunges at Callie for a hug, almost tackling her through the gate she came through. "You are here!" Callie screams. Nate leans down to grab her luggage and asks, "Is this all Shelby?" "Yes, thanks Nate," she says as she leans in to hug him. Callie loops her arm around Shelby's, "Okay, so tell me everything about your class." The entire ride back to Shelby's condo she tells them stories about the troublemakers in her class this year and how one student actually ate an eraser for ten bucks. "He's an eighth-grader Callie, as in going to High School next year. He's eating freaking erasers for money." The three laugh together as they pull up to the condo.

Shelby sighs and says in shock, "Wow! I forgot how beautiful this place is." Taking in the charm the condo held with its vibrant tropical potted flowers hanging from the porch as palm trees blew in the wind near the driveway. Looking around at the crisp white steps that led up to the narrow enclosed porch that linked all the condos together. Ruby gave her the same condo that she and Callie used last summer. The condo was set up in a cute duplex that sat back off the main road. It was in need of some updates, so Ruby hired Nate's company to do the work. She even let Nate and Callie live at a different condo down the road until their house was done. "So, are the Charleston's here?" Shelby asks. "Actually, they are not," Callie answers. "Their youngest daughter and her husband went on a trip, so they went to stay at their house to watch their two children." Shelby replies, "I bet they are loving that!". "Or not," Nate laughs. "The kids are teenagers and from the sound of it, they may be a bit on the wild side." Laughing, Shelby replies, "Oh boy, I bet Mr. Charleston is losing his mind!"

"So, it's just me here at the unit?" Shelby asks. Callie looks at Nate and then back to Shelby with a timid expression and says, "Well, that is what I was going to talk to you about." Shelby glances down the long porch to the door on the other side of the unit, when she notices a truck parked out front. It hit her all at once. Placing her hand over her chest as if she needed to calm her breaths, Shelby inhales deeply, hesitating before speaking. Quickly looking back at Callie, her eyes wide saying, "Please tell me it's not..." but her sentence was cut off as the other condo door opens. Gasping, Shelby steps back, tensing her hands at her side while looking down the porch. A man steps out, and not just any man. It was him. Liam.

Chapter 2

Liam knew he was going to see her. Nate had already told him she was coming to stay here for the summer. Nate knew there was something between Liam and Shelby, but Liam had never told him what it was. In fact, Liam had never really told him anything. Nate just assumed there was something there, but little did he know, there had been a little more than just something between them.

Liam, staring at Shelby thinks to himself, God, she's gorgeous and so tempting. There she stands, in front of him, wearing yoga pants, a John Legend t-shirt, and Converse shoes. Her hair in a messy bun thrown on top of her head, and her beautiful chocolate brown eyes just staring back at him. Looking her up and down he felt his senses tighten as his chest beat faster. "Hey, Shelby, good to see you again," Liam says casually. With a snarky tone, Shelby replies, "Hello Liam." The two just stand there staring at each other in silence. Both looking at the other with a sense of guilt and remorse. "How have you been?" He asks her. "I've been great. Really great." A sense of panic rolls through her but she tries to knock down the nerves before she speaks again. Shelby replies with a shaky tone. "How have you been?" She asks in return, just to make the conversation a little less awkward. "I've been good, thanks for asking. Nate has been keeping me busy with work, and I am helping out when I can on their house," Liam responds.

Turning to look at Callie with a death stare, Shelby replies, "I didn't know you were helping out on their house." "Yes, he's been a huge help for Nate. He is in and out with everything so fast. It has really helped speed up the progress on everything," Callie answers. "Well, glad to see he's helping someone," Shelby shot back in a sarcastic tone. Mumbling softly, but just loud enough to still be heard, Shelby replies, "In and out and gone must be his thing." Clenching his jaw, Liam glares at her remark, still standing in front of her. Narrowing her eyes at him, Shelby spins back around to head for the door to her condo. "Shelby!" Liam shouts as she turns to walk away. "Bye Liam, good to see you," she says walking into her condo not even giving him another glance. "Yikes! What did you do to her that you forgot to tell me?" Nate says to Liam as Callie follows Shelby through the door. Rolling his eyes and shaking his head, Liam replies as he rubs his hands through his tussled hair, "Not a thing. I think she's just jet-lagged." Nate throws back with a grin, "Yeah, jet-lagged from her three-hour flight."

"What was that?" Callie asks as she closes the door. "What was what?" Shelby replies. "The attack on Liam," Callie says. "I didn't attack him!" Shelby responds with attitude. "Then, what would you call that lovely greeting?" Callie asks her. "Let's just say we didn't really get along the last time we saw each other," says Shelby. "A little heads up that he was going to be here would have been nice." Callie hesitantly asks, "Why would it matter if Liam was here?" Shelby looks at Callie and replies, "It doesn't matter. I just would have liked to have known who I'd be staying with." Callie grins, "But you aren't staying with him. He's in his own condo and you are in yours." Shelby rolls her eyes at Callie, frustrated she even has to discuss this.

Callie sat down on the couch as Shelby looked out the window. "I know something happened last summer that you aren't telling me. I know you Shelby, and I know when something is up. You have asked me several times about Liam here and there. Did you not think I would put it together? Then, you get here today and act like that towards him?" Shelby spins around facing her friend. "Look, maybe something did happen, but it's not what you think and whatever happened was a mistake. I thought Liam was a really nice guy but turns out that's not the case," Shelby says with anger in her voice. "Callie, I don't think you really know him well enough to defend him."

Trying to keep the peace, Callie responds, "Shelby, you are my best friend, practically my sister. No matter who or what comes into my life, I will always defend you. I'm not trying to take sides here, but I know you can be stubborn, especially when it comes to guys. We both can be," Callie says smirking at Shelby. "I may not know him on a personal relationship level, but he has done nothing but help us out around here. When Nate needed him last summer, he was there. Don't you remember that day on the beach? If Liam would not have jumped at Paul while he was on the ground, who knows what would have happened with that knife," Callie says in a softer tone. Shelby looks down reliving the moment in her mind. "I know," she replies.

Nate walks in the room letting Shelby know the kitchen was fully stocked and everything in the condo was good to go. "All stocked up in the kitchen?" Shelby asks. "I may have gone grocery shopping for you and bought some of your favorites," Callie replies grinning at her. "You didn't have to do that," Shelby says. "I know, but I didn't want to waste any time we could have together," Callie replies with giddiness in her voice.

Shelby shot Nate a look with a smirk, knowing their summer plan was a go and Callie has no idea.

"Nate and I will be back to pick you up around 6:00 p.m.," Callie says as she throws her hands up with excitement. "The rehearsal dinner is at 6:30 p.m." Nate voices, "Liam actually just told me he would drive you, so we can all just meet there." Shelby's face immediately turns red and her eyebrows raise as she asks angrily, "What?" Callie cut her off. "No, we will come to get you," she replies. Nate looking confused, but replying, "Okay." Wrinkling her forehead in confusion, Shelby asks them, "Why is he coming to the rehearsal dinner?" Callie answers slowly, "Well, one of Max's groomsmen had a sudden death in his family. So, being that Max and Liam have gotten close over the last year, he asked him to fill in." With an astonished expression, Shelby says loudly, "Are you serious?" Both Callie and Nate look at Shelby stunned.

"Shelby, are you okay staying here near Liam? If there is something we should know, please tell us," Callie says sadly. Nate looks up scowling and asks, "Is there something maybe I should know?" Shelby stopped them both. "No, it's nothing too bad, just a mistake. Liam and I just, well, we actually..." She stops talking and puts her head down grinding her teeth as she fumbles with her hands. Red flushes up her neck as she swallows and blows out a deep sigh. Nate shot Callie a grin. "You two hooked up last summer, didn't you?" He said loudly. Callie's eyes grow big and her mouth drops open. "Oh, my God, Shelby, I knew it!" Callie says with excitement. Shelby glares at them, "Out!" she yells. "Shelby, what happened?" Callie asks with anticipation. "I'm not talking about it, and especially with either of you," she says. Nate still grinning, says, "See Cal, I told you they would be good together." Shelby replies sternly, "Stop! Both of you. Just stop. No, we are not good together. In fact, it was a disaster and I need you both to keep your mouths shut about it. No questions and no bringing it up again. As a matter of fact, just act like it never happened, because that's what I have done since I left last summer. I'll see you at 6:00 p.m. because I'm not riding with him." Noticing the sadness in her Shelby's tone, Callie drops her grin and replies more seriously, "Okay, see you soon." Grabbing Nate by the arm, they walked out the door.

Shelby sinks down into the couch, tears filling her eyes. Heavy with emotions she leans her head against the couch and begins to drift back to memories of last summer. That first moment she noticed Liam walking towards the table; she knew then he had the power to destroy her heart. Why was he here she thought to herself, why him? Shelby hears a knock at the door. Mumbling as she stands up to open the door. "I told you two, I don't want to talk about it anymore," stuttering as Liam appears in the doorway. Full of anger Shelby begins to push the door closed without saying a word to him. Liam catches the door, gripping it tightly saying, "Shelby, you have to talk to me at some point." Shelby replies harshly, "No, I don't." Liam pushes the door back open and says, "Shelby, I think we need to talk." Shelby replies hastily, "Nope, I have nothing to say to you, Liam." Liam responds nervously, "Shelby, you don't understand. You think you know what happened that night..." Shelby interrupts, "Liam, I think I remember just fine. Now, can you please go? I have to get ready." Thoughts begin to swirl in Shelby's mind taking her back to that night.

Leaning in closer to her, he reaches for her hand and says in a pleading tone, "Shelby, talk to me." Looking to Liam she sees the sorrow in his eyes, and the sadness in his tone. She wishes it could all be different, but he did this. She replies with resentment in her voice, "Don't touch me!" He flenches a bit at her comment but understands her resentment. Remembering back to last summer and how quickly she left him, not allowing him to explain anything. Liam replies with disgust, "Damn it, Shelby, let me in, please. We need to talk." Shelby then responds," Liam, can you please just leave me alone for the next two days? Then we can both go back to how things were before." Liam explains, "I can't do that Shelby." She says with disappointment in her eyes, "Well, you have to. This weekend is not about us. It's about Sophie and Max." Liam responds"I know that, but I want to explain. Shelby, I have not stopped thinking about you these past few months." She yells, throwing her hands to her side, "Stop! I'm not riding with you tonight either. Callie and Nate are picking me up." Narrowing his eyes at her he groans and then says with a smirk, "Fine, have it your way." Liam takes a step back from the door looking at her eyes, noticing the hurt that is present, dropping his shoulders he turns and walks towards his condo.

Standing on the other side of the door, Shelby puts her hands on her face and slides down the door. She hates him so much. She absolutely, positively, hates him. Throwing her head back, she lets out a deep sigh. She closes her eyes as a tear slips down her cheek. With each tear, another drops down her face. Thinking about her hatred for him, she begins to wonder, why does it hurt so bad to see him? Why do I want to kiss him so badly, if I hate him so much? She begins to cry harder, chills run through her body, and as she closes her eyes she buries her head in her knees. Her heart just shattered all over again.

Chapter 3

She makes me so angry. Thinking she knows everything and being so damn feisty. God, but she's so damn beautiful. Liam begins to pace back and forth across his condo while rubbing his face vigorously and thinks to himself, she has no idea about what happened last summer. With a deep sigh, rubbing his hand on his face and then around to the back of his neck, he says, "That is it. I'm going to prove her wrong." He knew from the first night they met at the bar last summer he wanted her. Walking up to the table, he remembers catching her eyes at the bar, and at that moment, he suddenly got the feeling he needed to talk to her. At first, Shelby and Liam were irritated with each other, which is what led them to more conversation throughout the night. Their deep conversations made him feel even more connected to her. He was used to people just going along with things and acting like everything was great. However, Shelby didn't put up with crap and his first impression of her intrigued him.

They had been in conversation most of the night when the two guys at the bar began to fight. Shelby got mixed up in the fists being thrown. As the men moved closer to where they sat, they accidentally knocked the table over. Liam was very protective of Shelby immediately. He had to restrain himself from beating both of the men up because they almost hurt her. The two men accidentally knocked Shelby on the floor amidst their fight. When Liam had reached her on the floor he found he couldn't let go of her. His rage was boiling, but he held on to her tight. Their breathing offbeat and his eyes locked on hers. He pulled her in close and carried her away from all the mess and chaos.

She had looked up at him thanking him as he pushed a piece of hair back out of her face, still looking at her. Again, he thought to himself, she was the most beautiful woman he had ever seen. A natural beauty, who didn't even know it. She was spunky and independent, but he knew she had a softer side. Running one hand through her hair and the other around her waist, he pulled her in and had asked, "Are you okay?" Both stood there in that moment, as if they never wanted it to end, still breathing heavily and feeling as if they were the only two people in the room. All the commotion and attention had brought the group back together. Each of them running up to Shelby asking what happened, which is the reason Liam suddenly lets Shelby go.

Liam closes his eyes and the memory begins to fade. He finds his mind starting to drift back to the present. Looking around his condo, he knew it would be hard to stay here again. Looking to the couch and then to the back bedroom, he thought of his first night with Shelby. The night that changed everything for him. He thought the night would have totally played out differently. Now, he couldn't even get himself to stay in the room they spent together. That room is different now because it is the room he last touched and kissed her in. He never wanted that night to end, until it did. He decides he is going to put his things in the smaller room across the hall instead. Groaning and shaking his head again, he walks to the bathroom to shower and get ready for the night.

"You look beautiful," Callie says as she looks at Shelby. Shelby curled her light brown hair and pulled half of it up with a clip. She is wearing a light purple, floral, maxi dress. The dress has a slit in the side, just high enough to show off her long legs, but still modest. The dress is a perfect sundress that flows as she walks, allowing it to be dressy enough for the dinner on the beach tonight. "Thanks, you too," Shelby says while looking at Callie's teal, long dress that fits tight on her curves. "How many dresses did you try on?" Shelby asks knowing how Callie is when she gets ready. "What makes you think I didn't have this one picked out and ready?" She says sarcastically. Shelby laughs and raises her eyebrows. "Fine, three! Now, let's go," Callie says, rolling her eyes. Chuckling, Shelby closes the door.

Sophie rushes to hug Shelby as soon as they walk up, saying "I'm so excited you are here!" Sophie leans in closer and whispers in Shelby's ear, "And that you'll be here for the summer too." Surprised, Shelby looks up at Sophie. "It's okay," Sophie says. "I was sworn to secrecy by Nate. He told me because he needed help keeping Callie busy the day he went to pick you up." Smiling Shelby says with a smirk, "I'm excited to spend all summer with you all. More importantly with the bride-to-be now." Pulling back from Sophie, Shelby greets Max as he walks up. Sophie throws her arms around Max and eagerly kisses her soon to be husband. Sophie shouts, "Can you believe it? All of us are back together and we are getting married tomorrow!"

Just then, Shelby senses someone staring at her. Glancing around over her shoulder, she sees Liam across the room standing in the doorway, with his gaze fixated on her. Shelby thinks to herself, wow, he looks so handsome. The two just stand there looking at one another. "Oh good, now we are all here," Sophie says, as she notices Liam approaching the group. Liam boasts, "Good evening everyone. Ladies, looking beautiful as always." Callie and Sophie giggle while Shelby says nothing. Liam's eyes still fixed on her with a grin on his face. "We better get to our seats. They are about to serve dinner," Max says. Callie wraps her arm around Nate and follows him to the table while motioning Shelby to sit by her. Shelby begins to follow when she sees Liam right behind her. The three sit down near Sophie and Max, followed by Liam, who finds an empty seat right across from Shelby. Just lovely, Shelby thought to herself. Looking up at Callie for help, Callie smirks and shrugs her shoulders.

While the group is enjoying their dinner, they all talk about work, life, and plans for the summer. Sophie and Max speak about their honeymoon and how they have four weddings this summer, all of which are out of town. Since last summer Sophie had hired a new manager for the shop. Sales were doing great and this allowed her more free time, which she desperately needed. Max had taken on a few new clients at his insurance firm since the renovations at the boutique were complete. Callie and Nate tell everyone about all the new renovations taking place on Ruby's duplex. Also, about how excited they are to wrap up their own house project.

"How is Ruby?" Shelby asks. "She is great," Callie replies. "Well, I wouldn't say great. She doesn't get around as she did before her fall last year. Also, she definitely doesn't take an easy on me that's for sure," Nate says with a chuckle. "Always a project being tossed on my plate," he further says. Callie laughs and says with a wink, "Yes, a project to keep you close to her, Nate." Nate leans in to kiss her and says, "I will always stay close." Shelby rolls her eyes, noticing Liam looking right at her.

"What are your plans for the summer?" Liam asks Shelby, as all eyes look in her direction. Caught up by his question she mumbles, "I am, well, I am planning to...," looking towards Nate for help. Nate's eyes grow wide. He looks at Callie, then back to Shelby. They had not really spoken about a cover story to hide their surprise from Callie. "I am teaching a summer science camp," she quickly lies. Callie looks at her with confusion. "I thought you hated those summer camps?" She says. "I do, but the money is good," Shelby replies. While looking at Shelby, Callie replies, "Do you think you can come to visit this summer?" Shelby sees the sadness in Callie's eyes, desperately wanting to tell her friend she would actually be here. However, knowing the surprise would be well worth it, she says, "I should be able to make two long weekend getaways work." Callie still looking sad, nods with a grin. "How about you Liam?" Sophie asks. Liam replies, "Actually, I'm still debating about that. I have a few options and an offer Nate has given me, but I haven't decided yet." Nate curiously looks at Liam and shakes his head with a smile.

After dinner, there is a dance on the beach. String lights hang forming a dance floor. Surrounding the dance floor are two mini bars and several black bistro tables. A small fire pit is located on the beach surrounded by chairs. The moon begins to glow off of the water and the waves hit the shore, creating a perfect backdrop. As the group moves outside, laughter fills the night sky. Music plays and the waves ripple in. Shelby sits alone around the fire, just staring out at the ocean. The breeze begins to pick up and just as she was rubbing her arms, a jacket falls around her shoulders. Startled, she looks up and sees it's Liam. "I thought you may be cold," he says as he sits down next to her. "Thank you. I am actually getting ready to see if Nate and Callie are ready to leave," she replies. Looking to the dance floor, pointing, he says, "I'm not sure if you'll get those two away from the dance floor anytime soon." Following his gaze, she sees Callie and Nate slow dancing. Callie rests her head on Nate's shoulder, while he rubs his hands down her back. "Ugh," Shelby groans. Liam chuckles. Shelby laughs and says, "Those two are so in love." Sitting back in his chair, Liam responds, "What's so wrong with that?" Shelby goes on and says, "Nothing is wrong with it. They are perfect. It's just love. Some people have it and others never will." Sitting up straight, Liam says while looking at Shelby, "Everyone can have love." Shelby questions, "Is that, right?" Liam replies, "Yeah it is. Love isn't something you are just given. It is something you find and hold on to." Rolling her eyes at him she looks back to the ocean.

"Do you not believe in true love or love at first sight?" He asks. Spinning her head back to Liam, she stares and begins to shrug the jacket off of her shoulders and lets it fall to the chair. "Thanks for the jacket Liam, but I am going to head home." Liam reaches for her wrist while she stands. "It was my sister," he says. "What?" She asks. "My sister. It was she I was talking to that morning." Shelby pulls her wrist away briskly and says, "I'm not talking about this here." "Fine, then can we talk about it at home?" Liam says. "No, we do not have a home," Shelby says with a snarky tone. Liam stands to meet her and says firmly, "Shelby!" While standing in front of Liam, he begins to explain, "My sister was in some kind of trouble and I was trying to help her. I missed her calls that night and was trying to call her back. It wasn't another girl, Shelby. It was family." Shelby begins to open her mouth to talk, but instead shakes her head and walks away.

As she gets a few feet away, Liam's voice echoes over the sandy beach, "It was real for me Shelby. I promise. If you would just listen..." Shelby turns around, now with tears in her eyes, she asks, "Why did you not tell me who it was then?" Liam responds softly, "You didn't give me a chance to. Then, you started ignoring me every time I saw you. Those next few days were absolutely crazy. I had to get stuff figured out with my sister back home. After I got back into town, the very next day was when the incident with Paul took place on the beach. Then, you had to leave to go back home." Shelby wipes away a tear. Liam begins to walk towards Shelby and she takes a few steps back. "Liam, we can't do this, and especially not here," she says quietly looking around. "Shelby, tell me you didn't feel anything, and I will leave you alone and walk away right now." Shelby just stands there, her heart beating out of her chest, and looks down as she turns around to head back inside.

Callie and Nate drop Shelby back off at her condo. Shelby walks ins and sits on her couch in silence, letting her thoughts run wild. An hour later, she hears a door close outside. Jumping up, she peeks out the window through the blind. It's him. She watches Liam walk to his door while he glances down to hers. Suddenly, he starts walking to her door. Letting go of the blind, she takes a step back and begins to hold her breath, wondering what he is going to do. Her heart begins beating even harder and her hands tremble with sweat. Then, all of a sudden, the footsteps stop. Liam hesitates, turns back around, and walks away. Shelby bursts into tears and wishes he would come back. Her emotions heavy, tears rolling down her cheeks, she thinks to herself, I was so wrong. She had been so focused on what he had done to her in the past, she kept filling her head with all the reasons to hate him. She had never really given him a chance to explain anything and hearing now that his sister was in trouble, she starts thinking back to that night. Shelby lays down in her bed, pulls the covers over her, and closes her eyes. She lets the pillow catch her tears.

The night they first met, Liam drove Shelby home from the bar. From the moment Liam walked up to the group at the bar, she felt a strong attraction to him. It worried her, but the connection she had to him was irresistible. She thought he had been so charming and funny, but also not too sure of himself. The two had talked all night, making each other laugh and feeling genuinely interested in the conversations they spattered back and forth. Silence had now filled the truck, both feeling nervous with anticipation, but also giddy at the same time. At times during their drive, they would look over to one another, soaking in each other's expressions and trying to read the other's thoughts. Shelby felt the heat radiate off them, feeling both desire and lust.

When Liam walked Shelby to her door, the two stopped and sort of just lingered, not wanting to call it a night yet. Shelby had been the one to go inside and close the door. Once she got inside, she realized she wanted him and didn't want the night to end. She wanted him so badly. She thought to herself, she just needed to see him one more time. When she had swung the door open and stepped back outside, she was shortly met by Liam as he was already beginning to walk back down the long porch towards her.

Her front door stood wide open as she anxiously awaited Liam to reach her. As soon as he got to her, he lifted her up into his arms, crashing his lips into hers. Backing up against the wall, she wrapped her arms around his neck and felt safe in his touch. He pulled her up, wrapping her legs around his waist. Then, began walking her back to his condo and closing the door behind them. As he made his way to the couch, he carefully lowered her and started kissing her even more passionately than she had ever been kissed before. So gently and ever so softly, he rubbed his hands on her back. Moving his lips from hers and down the side of her neck, he whispered, "Shelby, what do you want?" She told him, "You Liam, I want you." He picked her up and carried her to his room kissing her neck, nose, and lips. They spent the night tangled up in one another. Again, and again, not being able to get enough of one another. Spending hours talking and telling one another their dreams and goals. Leading to finally, falling asleep in each other's arms.

Shelby woke up to Liam on the phone in the next room. Startled by the conversation, she grabbed her clothes and began to put them on quietly. She heard him say, "I told you I would be back home in a few days. I've been working on a few things here. No, you don't need to come here, that will just cause more trouble. Just give me a few days to figure things out and I'll come home. I love you, too." When Shelby heard those last words, "I love you, too," her heart froze. She had never experienced love at first sight. However, that night with Liam made her heart skip a beat and gave her butterflies in her stomach. He was perfect for her, she thought to herself. Except now, she realized he must have been perfect for some-one else.

As Shelby busted through the bedroom door, Liam just hung up the phone and shot her a startled look. Tears began to fill Shelby's eyes and with an angry voice, she questioned, "Do you have a girlfriend or are you married? Oh, my God, why did you not say something?" She said frantically. Liam responds worriedly, "Shelby, let me explain." Shelby shouts, "No, I cannot believe I fell for you!" Shocked, Liam stood there trying to understand her words and what exactly was happening. "Fell for me?" He repeated. "Just forget it, Liam, and please forgive me for being so stupid! This never should have happened," she said running out the door and back to her room. He came down to her room several times that morning, knocking and begging her to open up and let him explain. Shelby never opened the door. In fact, she stayed there the remainder of the day and through the night. She came out of her room the following afternoon and realized his truck was gone. Callie had called a few times, but Shelby just said she had too much to drink and was trying to sleep it off.

The next day is when the accident took place and Shelby had been thrown to the ground. As the dust settled, Shelby began to open her eyes and realized Liam was the one who was holding onto her, protecting her. Shock suddenly set in from not only being thrown to the ground and hitting her head, but Liam being the one holding on to her. It completely took her words and breath away. As soon as the cops arrived, Shelby had left with Callie to head to the station for their testimonials about Paul. The next day, she stayed with Callie, leaving the summer behind her the following day.

Chapter 4

Shelby opens her eyes to a ringing alarm and sun shining into the room. Instantly, she realizes it is Sophie's wedding day! She jumps up to take a shower and waits for Callie to pick her up. She notices Liam's truck is gone when Callie picks her up., but quickly shakes the thought of him out of her mind. The bridal party spent the morning getting their hair and nails done. Afterward, the bridesmaids begin to help Sophie prepare to walk down the aisle.

The ceremony turned out perfectly, and Sophie is such a stunning bride. Watching Sophie and Max stare at one another, Shelby realizes how deep their love is for one another. In the back of her mind, she has hope that she, too, will find love as strong as theirs one day. As Sophie and Max say their written vows to one another, Shelby catches Liam staring at her, with sadness in his eyes, but hope in his demeanor. Suddenly, her heart feels as if it dropped to her stomach. She gazes back at Liam, but then quickly glances the other way. Shelby thinks to herself, thank goodness, she didn't have to walk down the aisle with Liam. Instead, she walked with one of Sophie's cousins.

After the ceremony, everyone heads to the reception. The reception is absolutely gorgeous. Vases of beautiful pink and red roses fill the tables. A combination of tea light candles and square mirrors surround the vases. The warm candle glow reflects off of the mirrors, dimly lighting the space. String lights hang around the area, creating a romantic ambiance. Lanterns filled with sand and seashells line the walkways and tiki torches glisten on patios and balconies.

Once dinner is served, the Maid of Honor and Best Man give their heartfelt, but funny speeches, which fills the room with laughter. As the crowd of people makes their way to the dance floor, Nate approaches Callie and Shelby. Shelby, who is sitting down with Callie chatting, takes a sip of her glass of wine when Nate reaches out and grabs Callie for a dance. Shelby smiles, as the two slip away to the dance floor. Finishing her drink, Shelby gets up and begins walking across the floor to get another glass of wine. She just about makes it through the crowd of people, when Sophie's cousin slips a hand around her waist, asking, "Will you dance with me, pretty lady?" Laughing, Shelby replies, "Well, I guess I have to now." He pulls her close to him and puts his hands on her hips, while she places her hands around his neck. The two begin to sway to a slow song.

Leaving the bar, Liam looks at the dance floor, anger now filling his body. He didn't know it would hurt this bad to see her with another guy. He is miserable, as he stares at her dancing with someone else. "You better go get your girl," Max teases, as he stands at the bar with Liam. "What? She's not my girl." Liam says, looking at Max oddly. "Whatever man, keep telling yourself that. We all see what you two won't let in," Max says, as he nudges Liam on the arm as he walks away. Liam watches Sophie's cousin Ted pull Shelby closer to his chest and lower his hands on her back. Growing even more irritated, Liam keeps trying to look away. As Ted lowers his hands farther down Shelby's back, Liam mumbles to himself while slamming down his drink, "That's it!" Nate whispers to Callie, "Here comes trouble." The two just casually watch what was about to play out across the dance floor.

"What are your summer plans?" Ted asks Shelby. Just as she begins to answer, she is interrupted by Liam who is now standing next to them. "Hey, I'm going to cut in if that's okay?" Liam says to Ted, grabbing Shelby's hand away from his before he can even answer. Shelby loosens her hold from Ted and slowly moves towards Liam as he pulls her to him. Ted shoots Liam a look, then turns away and heads towards the bar.

Shelby is in complete shock about what just happened. She doesn't know what to say but just stands there not wanting to make a scene in the middle of the dance floor. "Why did you do that," she whispers with frustration. "He was getting grabby and I saved you," Liam responds. "Ha! Saved me? No, Liam, you didn't save me, you just helped yourself to what you wanted." Shelby replies hastily. Dropping her hands from his and taking a step back, Shelby begins to feel lost. "Shelby, please, just one dance," Liam begs as they stand still looking at one another. Glancing around at everyone on the dance floor watching them, Shelby sighs and murmurs, "Fine, one dance."

Liam smiles and wraps his arms around her, pulling her closer to him. Why does it feel so good to be in his arms, Shelby thinks to herself. Staring into her eyes, Liam says, "You look absolutely beautiful tonight, Shelby" Blushing, Shelby replies, "Thank you, and you look okay, too, I guess?" Liam laughs and questions, "Just okay?" With a smirk, Shelby says, "Yeah, just okay." Liam apologetically says, "Shelby, I really am sorry about everything," Her voice soft and honest, replies, "Don't, please not here. Let's just enjoy this dance and get through the night, okay?" Quietly, Liam replies, "Okay, I can do that." The two dance and just as she closes her eyes to convince herself she can make it through this song, Liam rubs her back gently, and her mind escapes to that first night they had together last summer. Sinking into his touch with the memories filling her mind, she lets herself go a little and withdraws the tension she feels, just for a moment.

Opening her eyes, Shelby realizes the music changed from a slow song to a faster one. Callie and Nate come jumping near them. "Throw your hands up and shout!" Callie screams, singing along to the song. Shelby lets go of Liam, embarrassed, and not sure how long they were standing there holding each other after the song ended. "Dance guys!" Nate yells, grabbing Callie and throwing her hands up. "You two are crazy and perfect for each other," Shelby says chuckling as she walks off the dance floor. Callie laughing, responds, "Yes we are!" Nate and Callie keep dancing the night away.

Shelby walks outside to get some fresh air. She looks out over the balcony towards the ocean, feeling a sense of relief as she watches the waves hit the shore. Her mind is replaying the dance with Liam. His touch, his voice, it all made her swoon. Suddenly, she hears footsteps walk up behind her, desperately hoping it isn't Ted. Just then, Liam appears. Closing the gap between them, Liam steps in front of her, lifting his hand to push a hair back behind her ear that the wind had caught. "Shelby, I need to tell you something," he says timidly. Quickly, Shelby puts her hand up signaling for him to stop talking and says, "No, let me speak first, please. Liam, I am so sorry I didn't give you a chance to explain, and I'm sorry I have been so hateful towards you this weekend." Liam steps closer without moving his hand from her face now and replies, "Shelby, don't apologize. If anyone should, it's me. I know it sounded bad to you that morning last summer. Looking back, I should have tried harder to tell you what was going on. I was just mad that morning with my sister. Then, you were ignoring me, so I simply gave up and left," he says sadly. Shelby's lip begins to tremble and she feels herself stepping in closer to his touch. "Shelby, I'm crazy about you. I've thought about you so much this past year." Liam whispers as he leans in softly to kiss her lips, "I've missed you so much." His lips are soft against hers and she feels goosebumps erupt throughout her. Shelby throws her arms around Liam's neck and he pulls her in closer for another kiss.

The passion from the kiss fades, as Shelby remembers she is leaving tomorrow. Every time they start to get close, Shelby's apprehensive thoughts always seem to get in the way. Thinking of his words, "gave up" she quickly pulls back from him. "What's wrong?" He asks. "We can't do this, Liam," Shelby groans. "Why not?" He asks with confusion filling his tone. "I'm leaving tomorrow and so are you," Shelby explains. "Shelby, but that's what I want to tell you..." Liam tries to reply, but Shelby interrupts, "Liam, we aren't good for each other." Anger, now in his voice, "What? Why would you say that? We haven't even tried. Look at us Shelby, we can't stay away from each other, and now you are saying we aren't good together?" Frustrated, Shelby replies, "Liam, you don't understand. This isn't real. What Nate and Callie, and Sophie and Max, have is real. A real connection." Liam's face went blank. "A real connection?" he questions with disappointment. "So, this thing we have been doing, just games, right?" He asks. "Games?" Shelby questions. "Yes, just a game, Shelby. It's all just a game to you. You are so..." His words trailing off, not finishing his thought. "What!" She yells at him. "I am so what, Liam?" The two, now standing far apart, scowl at one another. "We aren't good for each other. All we do is fight and say hurtful things to each other," Shelby says.

Liam, softening his gaze, replies, "No, Shelby, it is you. You're the one that causes the hurt." Liam turns around and walks away from her. Shelby's shoulders move up and down, and she tries to catch her breath as she watches Liam walk-through back through the door and away from her. Closing her eyes, she wipes her tears thinking about the amazing kiss they just shared and how incredibly hollow she now feels.

The next morning, Callie and Nate pick Shelby up to take her to the airport. She had not seen or heard Liam's truck pull into the condo last night. Instantly, filled with sadness and regret, Shelby's heart breaks at the thought of Liam going home for good. Trying to shake the bad thoughts away, she keeps telling herself, it all happened for a reason. "I'll see you soon, I hope," Callie says to Shelby, as she hugs her one last time. Shelby smiles and replies, "Sooner than expected, hopefully." Shelby begins to smirk secretly at Nate.

Chapter 5

"Okay, Nate, so you really think she has no clue?" Shelby asks. "No, I don't think she suspects anything. She actually got mad at me because I have been trying so hard to finish the house and have hardly been home. I almost have it finished, but Ruby said you are welcome to stay in the condo as long as needed. When I finish up with the house you can stay with us," he says proudly. Shelby laughs and replies, "I really may just stay at the condo this summer if that's okay. I know Callie would love the nightly sleepovers, but I have a feeling you, not so much." Nate chuckles and replies with a grin, "Thanks, Shelby, but you are always welcome to stay with us."

Nate pulls his truck into the driveway of the duplex. As Nate gets out of the truck, Shelby finds herself looking towards the last unit, where Liam had stayed. Pausing, she feels her heartache for him, wondering where he is, and what he is doing now. "He's not here. Actually, he was going to help me with a side job this summer, but he turned me down about a week ago. He said something came up and he was leaving for a while," Nate says breaking her thoughts. Shelby sighs, "Why did he turn you down?" Hesitantly, Nate replies, "I'm not really sure. He had pretty well already committed to me, but then a few days after Max and Sophie's wedding he changed his mind.

I told him you would be here this summer." Shelby frowns looking at Nate and says, "I'm sorry if I caused you to miss out on a job." With a coy smile, Nate replies, "Why would you have anything to do with that?" In a defeated tone, Shelby says, "Nate, come on, I know Callie tells you everything. Liam and I had a fight the night of the wedding and now all of a sudden he's not here to help you." While tossing Shelby's luggage on the front porch, Nate exclaims, "It's no big deal, honestly, I can do it alone. It will just take me a bit longer. Besides, I will have all the spare time I need once Callie sees you are here." Shelby laughs and giddiness now filling her voice, replies, "She's going to freak out!" After Nate and Shelby unload her things, the two head off for Callie and Nate's new house.

Sophie takes Callie to the store to help pick out some new furniture, as Sophie was needing to distract Callie until Shelby's arrival. Callie and Sophie pull up to Callie's house and Nate runs out to help carry in a few shopping bags. "Hey babe, did you save anything for anyone else?" Nate says as he grabs the bags from Callie. Callie laughs and replies, "Nope, I bought it all." Stepping out onto the porch with a huge smile, Shelby boasts, "Well damn, if there's nothing left for me, I guess I should go back home!" Excitement, screams, and laughter fill the front porch, and within seconds Callie leaps up the steps and hugs Shelby. Callie screams with joy and asks, "What are you doing here?" After Shelby explains she is going to be here for the summer, the four of them meet Max for drinks. They spent the evening catching up and chatting about all the things they could do during the summer.

Looking around at all the couples enjoying their night, Shelby suddenly feels a sense of loss. Like a piece of her was broken. Liam didn't mean anything to her. He was just another guy who ended up being a roadblock. At least, that is what she tells herself. Thoughts of the two of them enter her mind. She begins to think about his touch, the way he used to kiss her, and overall just the way he made her feel. A smile begins to illuminate across her face, as she thinks back to how Liam knew exactly what to say to make her swoon all over him. Further, deeper into thought, she thinks about how they spent such a small amount of time alone together, and yet how instantly they became connected.

Shelby stands up and announces, "I'm going to the restroom, I'll be right back." Walking out of the restroom, she accidentally drops her phone on the ground. While bending over to pick it up, she hears a man's voice. "Well, hello there," the voice says seductively. Turning around annoyed, she unexpectantly sees a familiar face. "Ted! Hey! How are you?" She shouts with a smile. Ted approaches her, leans in for a hug, and says, "Much better now!" Shelby laughs, remembering he had no filter the last time they spoke. "I'm actually here with Sophie," Shelby replies. Ted motions towards the bar and says, "Great! Let's get around for everyone and I'll join the party if that's okay with you?" Shelby replies, "Of course." How polite of Ted to ask before he joins the party, Shelby thinks to herself. That is something Liam would have never done. Liam is just so direct and tends to do things his way. The two join the group and conversations carry on throughout the night.

"Ted seems really nice," Callie says with a wink. "Yes, he is," Shelby replies. "Sophie said he will be here on and off this summer. He's helping them with their financial expansion plans," Callie reports. Sophie and Max decided to try to expand the boutique into more than just clothing. Shelby slowly says, "Okay... and your point?" Callie laughing, replies, "No point, just small talk." Shelby crosses her arms, glares at Callie, and remarks, "There is no small talk with you Callie."

Over the next few days, Callie and Shelby go to the beach to relax and enjoy the warm summer air and catch up on all the gossip from back home. "So, dinner out tonight?" Callie asks. "Sounds perfect!" Shelby replies. "Great, Sophie and Max will be joining us, too. I told Sophie to invite Ted as well. He's in town and it would be rude to not include him, don't you think?" Callie says grinning sheepishly. Shelby rolling her eyes, responds, "Callie, seriously, stop trying to play cupid. I am here this summer to enjoy the beach and you only. No men. No drama." Callie now laughing and walking out of her condo questions, "Isn't that what you said last summer?"

Later that night the group went to eat at one of Shelby's favorite restaurants for dinner, *The Hot Steamer*. The restaurant sits right on the beach near the marina. At dusk, one can not only see the amazing sunset but also see the boats pulling back into the marina after a long day of fishing. The back of the restaurant has a beautiful patio surrounded by palm trees and twinkling strand lights dangling from each palm tree. The music is light during dinner hours, but the bar outside attracts a crowd for the late-night entertainment. The group opts to eat outside, as there is a light breeze to help prevent them from getting too hot. Dinner is going great and Ted seems to be getting along with everyone well, too. He is making jokes and carrying on as if he has known them all for years. He even shares some common interests with Shelby and Max, regarding scientific research and environmental awareness. Shelby, to say the least, is very impressed by Ted.

The night they shared on the dance floor when they first met Shelby saw his eager, free spirit side. Tonight, she sees someone who could be fun company throughout the summer. Definitely, does not resemble Liam even in the slightest bit.

Ted and Liam couldn't be more opposite to one another. Liam is extremely handsome, yes, but also smooth and laid back. Ted on the other hand is sophisticated, charming, and good looking. Liam tends to be rude, while Ted is nothing but nice. Shelby thinks to herself, well not completely rude, just rude to her when they bickered. The night is flying by. As dinner comes to a finish and all their drinks are gone the group begins to disperse home.

Sophie and Max disappear, followed shortly by Nate and Callie. "Are you coming with us?" Callie asks Shelby. "Yes!" Shelby answers a little too quickly. She goes on to say, "I mean, yes, I am pretty tired and should probably call it a night." Callie and Nate say goodbye to Ted and head for their truck. Ted pauses, grabbing Shelby's hand at the door. Smiling, he says, "Shelby, I would really like to take you out one night while I am here." Shelby thinks to herself, what could it hurt, he seems nice and charming. "Not a date though, right?" she asks. Ted hesitantly replies, "No, let's make it a *getting acquainted with the town* kind of night." Shelby laughs and replies, "Okay, well, when you put it that way I'd love to." Ted smiling says, "You know any good hole in the wall places? I'll let you pick where we eat. I'll come by your place tomorrow to pick you up at 6 p.m., sound good?" Shelby replies, "Yes, sounds perfect." Shelby reassures herself, it's not a date.

Pulling up to the condo, Shelby decides to not tell Callie until tomorrow about her and Ted's friends-only dinner night out. I can't handle her reaction this late, Shelby thinks to herself. Shelby gasps as Nate's truck stops in front of her condo. All eyes now on the truck that sits parked outside Liam's old condo. Callie in shock looks to Nate. Nate explains, "Yeah, I may have forgotten to tell you...Liam texted me this morning about coming back. He still had the key from his last visit, so

I told him he could just stay there. Sorry, Shelby, I wasn't sure if he would really come, so I didn't want to tell you yet. I definitely didn't think he would come today. Honestly, I thought it would be another week or so. I was hoping I would have another week that way the house would be done and you could just stay with us if you wanted."

Shelby opens the door stepping out grumbling, "It's fine. I'm not avoiding him or letting him ruin my summer." Callie frowning says, "Shelby, do you want me to..." Cutting her off before she finishes her question, Shelby says, "Really guys, it's fine. No big deal, it's just Liam. Besides, we both know we are not good for each other and we are adults. We can handle staying next to each other for a few days." Nate inhales deeply and nervously replies, "Yeah, it's actually going to be the rest of the summer, maybe a bit longer. He accepted my side job offer, so he'll be here longer than a few days." Callie grunts and shoots Nate a look. Shelby puts her head down, groans, and heads for her door. Shelby hears Callie and Nate bickering in the truck as she closes the condo door behind her.

Chapter 6

The next morning, Shelby gets up early to go on a run. She purposely woke up before the sunrise, so she could try to avoid Liam in hopes that he would be gone before she got back. Popping her earbuds in, she opens the door slowly looking towards Liam's truck, and then towards his door. Why am I being so crazy? This is nuts, she tells herself. Quietly closing her door, she heads down the road to clear her mind of all the crazy Liam drama. I am going to enjoy the summer. I am going to make new friends. And most of all, I am going to avoid Liam. Shelby thinks to herself repeatedly during her run.

Running back towards her condo, she sings to herself and thinks about the Sea Festival that Callie mentioned earlier in the week. The Sea Festival is a huge carnival hosted on the beach every summer. There are food trucks, games, and local vendors throughout the week, and a dance is held at the beach on the last night of the festival. During the day hours, the festival offers jeep rides on the beach, horseback riding through some of the sandy shores, and several other fun activities for the locals and tourists to enjoy. People come from all around to visit the festival. It has become a new tradition over the last few years that the community has grown to love. Stopping in her tracks, Shelby comes to a halt. There, leaning against his truck is Liam with his arms crossed and a smile on his gorgeous face. Pulling her earbuds out of her ears and dropping them to her chest, she stares at him. She doesn't even know what to say. She had been so focused on the festival that she hadn't even thought to look up towards his condo. Her heart begins to beat even faster, and all at once, she feels as if she might get sick. She stumbles a bit, still staring at him, but quickly turns back around to run the other way.

"Hey, are you okay? You look really pale Shelby," Liam says to her. "Yes, I am fine. I went for a long run, just tired," she replies annoyed. Liam begins to walk towards her, but Shelby picks up her pace and heads towards her condo. She turns her head towards her door and focuses on just making it to her unit before he could say anything else. "Shelby! Hey, Shelby, can we talk?" he asks. Liam starts to trail behind her, his steps getting closer. Shelby stops, whips around, and with her eyes narrowed says, "Liam, we have nothing to talk about. I think we said enough last time." Liam just stares at her. "No, I think you said what you wanted," he replies frustrated. Shelby tilts her head and says with a smirk, "Exactly, I said what I thought was best." She pushes open her door and slams it shut in his face.

Liam sits on his porch thinking to himself wondering what he could do or say to change her mind. He knows he screwed up and tried to fix it, but she didn't want to. Why do I want her so badly? She drives me crazy, he thinks to himself. She is so stubborn and hot-headed, but damn, I love it. She is so independent and sexy, too, that's for sure. He rubs the back of his neck with his hand wondering how he could ever make this right.

Nate asks through the phone, "Hey man, how is it going? Do you want to head over here tonight? I'm trying to finish up some wires on this electrical box. You can help me out and we can have a few drinks afterward." Replying through the phone Liam answers, "I'll be over there in a bit." Nate chucking replies, "How is your neighbor?" Liam laughs, "Is that even a question?" Liam hangs up the phone and walks out to his truck. As he tosses his tool bag in the back, he sees a black sports car pull into the drive. Parking outside of Shelby's condo, the door opens and Ted steps out. Fists tight, Liam feels like he had just been kicked in the gut. He mutters to himself, "What the hell?" Starting the truck, but not moving, he sees Shelby walk outside towards the car. She looks beautiful all dressed up. Ted meets her halfway and places his hand on her back to help her to the car. Shelby's eyes catch Liam's just as she gets in the car. The hurt in Liam's eyes makes Shelby feel ashamed and she wonders if this really is a good idea after all.

Ted closes the door behind her, and as he turns to walk around the car, he looks up at Liam and smiles. Instantly, Liam thinks of how he could smash Ted with just one punch. Ted thinks this is a competition, Liam thinks to himself. Liam's fingers have a death grip on the steering wheel. His grip so tight, his knuckles begin to turn white. His breathing uneven and his heart in pieces. The car drives away and Liam does everything he can to not follow them.

"So, she went out with Ted? When did that happen?" Nate asks. "I'm not sure, but you could have told me," Liam replies angrily. Nate looks up saying, "Seriously, I didn't know. Besides, Callie didn't say anything to me about that. He must have asked her when we were all at dinner. I don't know when else it could have been. Unless they've been hanging out...sorry man, I shouldn't have said that" Nate apologizes when he catches the defeated look on Liam's face. Liam drops his head saying, "It's fine. She deserves someone good, and she's already told me how she feels anyways. He can have her if it makes her happy." Nate looks up at his friend sighing, "Do you expect me to really believe that?

Look, I will tell you this. She was upset that you were gone when she got here." Liam asks, "What do you mean?" He perks up instantly. "When I dropped her off at the condo after getting her from the airport that day, she was expecting you to be there. She actually apologized to me for chasing you off. Look, I think she cares for you, a lot. And take it from me, if you like her, then you need to fight for her. Shelby is a good girl, Liam, and I care a lot about her, too. She has always been there for Callie, even when I wasn't. Don't let a guy like Ted take your girl," Nate says with a smirk just before tossing Liam a tool. Catching the tool, Liam smiles back at him. "Thanks, man. Now let's get these damn wires figured out so I can go home," Liam joked.

Chapter 7

Ted insists on walking Shelby to the door, even though Shelby reminded him this was just a night out as friends. "Dinner was so nice. Thank you, Ted," Shelby says as they get out of the car. "I'm so glad you enjoyed the evening. So, when can we go on a real date?" Ted asks as they reach Shelby's condo door. Shelby smiles and replies, "Ted, you are so sweet. I really appreciate you taking me out tonight, but I just want to enjoy this summer. I am not looking for anything serious right now." Ted places his hand on her cheek and whispers softly as he moves closer to her, "Who said anything about getting serious, Shelby? We can take it slow and just have fun."

Shelby hears a loud noise behind them. Jumping back, she catches Liam out of the corner of her eye. "Sorry," Liam says as he drops his tool bag at his doorstep. Ted drops his hand to his side and glares over his shoulder at Liam down the long porch, refusing to break the distance between him and Shelby. "Where did you come from?" Shelby yells at Liam over Ted's shoulder. "Around back. I've been working at Nate's and was just putting something up, about to head in for the night," Liam answers. Shelby rolls her eyes at him.

Ted grabs Shelby's hand, but she quickly shakes it off. Her eyes blazing in Liam's direction, who is still standing at his door and fumbling with his keys. Shelby turns to look at Ted and says, "Goodnight, and thank you, again." Liam, now kneeling down, is messing with his tool bag on his doorstep. "I'll call you when I get back in town in a few days. Remember, think about what I asked, okay?" Ted says to her with a soft smile. Shelby grins hesitantly at him, knowing Liam is still listening. "Thanks again, Ted," Shelby says. Opening the front door, she steps inside and shuts the door. Ted begins to head down the steps towards his car. "See you later, Liam. Keep an eye on my girl, okay?" Ted says, full of arrogance. Liam glares at Ted in anger. He thinks to himself how badly he would like to knock Ted out. However, he knows then his chances with Shelby would lessen even more.

Minutes later, Shelby watches Ted pull away and opens her door, ready to confront Liam, but stops when she steps outside. He is already walking halfway to her door. "What are you doing, Liam?" Surprised to see her, he stops too. "What do you mean?" he questions. "Were you walking to my door?" Shelby asks him with an attitude, crossing her arms. "Where were you going?" he asks her. "I was...I was walking around back to sit on the gazebo," she lies. "Ha!" Liam laughs. "You are lying!" Shelby scrunches her nose and curls her hands into fists. "Do you like to fight with me? Confrontation is so your thing!" She yells at him. Liam walks closer, grunting, "What are you doing going out on a date with Ted?" Shelby shoots back, "That is none of your business. Besides, why are you back here, Liam?" Liam looks right at her, hesitating before answering softly, "I came back because you are here."

Feeling her stomach turn and twist, Shelby replies, "Liam, do not lie to me." Liam replies bitterly, "Shelby, I came back because Nate said you would be here this summer and I couldn't stand the thought of you being here alone. Shelby, I know you said you don't want me or think we are good together, but you have not even given us a chance. I come back, and now Ted is worth giving a shot? He's not even your type." Laughing, Shelby questions, "He's not my type?" She laughs even harder now. "So, what is my type, Liam? You?" She asks crossing her arms and pursing her lips. Liam gradually moves his hand onto her shoulder and begins to caress her arm, replying, "Yes, I do think I am." His unexpected remark catches her off guard, allowing the silence to fill the space between them.

"Liam, I don't think so!" She says as she shrugs her shoulder away from his touch. "I'm going to prove to you that we are good for each other," he says softly. Shelby just stands there staring at him, now more upset looking than angry. "How are you going to do that?" She argues. Liam touches her cheek with his thumb and begins to move his hand down her jawline to her chin and remarks in a snarky tone, "You can try to keep pushing me away from you, but answer this...why are you out here with me when you just got home from a date?" Shelby groans and shakes his hand away. "You are something else, aren't you? Am I just a sport to you?" She yells back at him. Liam looking confused asks, "A sport?" "Yes, you know, you saw him dropping me off so you purposely ran him off. It's like a competition for you." Angry at her comment, Liam starts to shake his head from side to side and grits his teeth. "You've probably been watching for me all night," she says putting her hands on her hips. Liam chuckling says, "Yes, actually I was." Shelby yells back, "Liam, you are so frustrating!" She pushes him, but Liam catches her hands and pulls her to him tightly against his chest. Holding her hands, their faces inches apart, Shelby looks into his eyes and develops butterflies in her stomach. Her breathing turns eratic while her heart pounds loudly in her chest. Liam kisses her nose, and as she closes her eyes, Shelby finds herself letting go of her anger and forgets what they were even arguing about.

Shelby thinks to herself this is why he is so dangerous for her. He knows how to make her so weak. Liam leans in, whispering in her ear, "You are beautiful, Shelby. It made me sick to see another man take you out. I'm sorry, but it's too hard to watch. If he is who you want, then tell me right now. I'm ready to fight for you, even if there is only a small chance for us." Shelby sighs and says so softly with remorse, "Liam." Liam leans in, kissing her cheek and then her neck. Shelby begins to wrap her arms around him, pulling her head back as he kisses his way up the side of her neck. Her eyes open wide as she realizes what is happening and abruptly pushes him back. "We can't, I'm so sorry. I can't do this. I want to do this, but I just can't," she says while taking a step back and pulling away from him with tears in her eyes.

Liam steps closer to Shelby as she continues stepping backward, brushing her back into the wall. "Shelby, please? We can go slow, don't push me away," he pleads. "Liam, you don't understand. It all ends the same way. We come from different places and may not even want the same things. We already have odds against us," she says sadly unable to look up at him. "Shelby, you don't know that. I will do whatever it takes to make us work, I promise," he says. Grabbing her quickly, he pulls her towards him, lifting her head up and kisses her. Shelby melts into his chest. He laces his hands around her neck, feeling as if he cannot get close enough. Shelby gives in, loving the feeling when he holds her like this. She also loves when they aren't fighting, and instead open and honest with each other.

Pushing her completely against the wall, Liam holds her face in his hands and puts his forehead to hers. "Shelby, hang out with me tonight, just for a little bit. Just a movie, a drink, or we can go somewhere to talk. Nothing else. I just want to be near you. I want us to figure out where this can go. I know you have that same gut feeling that I do. I can see in your eyes that you want me, too," he says passionately. Letting out a deep sigh Shelby feels herself letting go of her raw emotions and opening up to the idea of him. Shelby places her hands on his sexy, muscular chest. Smiling, she replies, "Okay, what if we just go for a drive?" Liam kisses her again, grabs her hand, and begins to walk her to his truck briskly. "Liam, let me go inside to change," Shelby says pulling back from his hand. "Not a chance," he replies looking her up and down. "You are driving me crazy in that dress! You are totally keeping that on so I can stare at those long legs all night. Plus, I am not letting you step a foot in that condo, giving you the opportunity to change your mind about going with me." Shelby's blushes after his comment and quickly covers her face with her other hand.

Opening the truck door, he helps her in and quickly jogs around to the other side of the truck. "Shelby, you are so beautiful," he says again as he stares at her before starting the truck. Grinning, she replies, "You already told me that tonight once, so you can kill the charm. Just drive before I do change my mind!" Now, she smirks at him with lust in her eyes and hopes she did not just make a mistake.

They drive around for almost two hours just talking to one another. They stop at an ice cream shop on the boardwalk. Liam parks towards the back of the parking lot, where they could still see the lights from the beach club overlooking the ocean. "I should have brought a blanket. I know you are cold," he says to her as they sit on the tailgate of his truck. "It's actually not too bad, a little breezy though," Shelby replies. Liam stands up, wrapping his arms around her. "I have something to tell you," he says taking a deep breath. Shelby moves her head back to look at him, curiosity growing. "What?" She asks shyly. Liam explains, "I was so jealous tonight when I saw Ted picking you up. I was even more jealous when I saw him dropping you off. I had been sitting in my truck waiting for you to get back." Sternly, Shelby says, "Liam!" Laughing he replies, "What? I wasn't about to let him put his hands all over you again. The wedding was bad enough." Shelby raises her eyebrows and says, "Well, you stopped that too, didn't you?" Thinking of how glad she was that he had.

"Liam, I have something to tell you," she says. "Ted may have thought tonight was more than just friends hanging out, but I didn't. I don't want him, Liam. I want you." Liam presses his mouth against hers. As soon as the words leave her mouth, she feels so much passion and heat in his kiss. Shelby laces her hands around his neck. Liam then pushes into her body as she wraps her legs tighter around him. Standing in front of her as she sits on his tailgate, the two kiss for what seems like hours, reminiscing about the last time they were together.

The entire ride back to the condo, the two couldn't stop looking at one another. "Liam, keep your eyes on the road," she says with a giggle. Flustered, he says with a sly grin, "I can't!" Pulling up to the condo, he turns off the truck and the two just sit there in silence, lost in their affection for one another. Liam takes a deep breath and says, "Shelby, I really want to come inside with you, but I also really want to prove to you that I am a good guy." Leaning in, she kisses him gently. "Liam, thank you," she says mischievously, just before leaping up and over the console of the truck to straddle him. Surprised, he gasps, "Shelby, what are you doing?" Grinning teasingly, Shelby says, "Well, if you aren't coming in, then I guess we need to sit out here like two young teenagers and make out like crazy before I go in for the night." Liam throws his head back laughing, thinking about this girl he had completely fallen for. Seductively raising his eyebrows, they move even closer now, feeling the heat radiate off each other's' bodies. Liam grins and then kisses her intensely.

Chapter 8

Looking at the time on her phone, Shelby lays her head back on her pillow and thinks about last night. A smile quickly spreads across her face, but a hint of worry begins to settle in. What am I doing she asks herself? While changing into her running clothes, she hears a loud noise outside. Walking to the window to peek out she sees Liam, wearing only grey beach shorts and a white V-neck, tossing a cooler into the back of his truck. Just seeing him gives her butterflies and makes her weak at the knees. She thinks to herself, damn, he's so hot and it's only 7 o'clock in the morning. It's not even normal to be that good-looking so early! Oh, crap, Shelby says dropping the curtain and realizing he is staring back at her. Embarrassed, she leans against the wall catching her breath as if she had just been caught stealing something. She begins to giggle to herself. Hearing footsteps and then a light knock at her door, her eyes open wide knowing she is busted. Rubbing her hands through her hair and pulling her T-shirt down farther to her knees, she opens the door.

"Good morning," Liam says standing in her doorway with a smile that makes her fall for him all over again. "Good morning," she replies shyly. After his eyes roam up and down her body, he asks, "Do you sleep in that?" She looks down, realizing she has on a light blue Johnny Cash T-shirt that barely covers her thighs and is borderline see-through from all the times she has washed it. "Yes, I do...I mean, I did. I love Johnny Cash, are you not a fan?" She questions. "I am now!" He replies with a grin. Blushing, she attempts to cover herself up more.

"What are you doing up so early?" Shelby asks. "I was waiting for you. Besides, I'm always an early bird, unless the night before gets the best of me," he replies. "Are you running today?" He asks her. "Actually, I was just about to get dressed to go for a run. Why?" Shelby demands. Liam looking down nervously asks, "Would you want to join me at the beach instead?" "Now!?" She exclaims. "Yes, the early bird gets the worm, or shells in our case," he replies. A huge smile appears on Shelby's face. She has not searched for seashells in years. "Yes, I would love that!" Liam says excitedly, "Great! I've got a cooler packed with some snacks and mesh bags for the shells." Pausing at those words, she asks slowly, "You really were waiting for me, weren't you?" Stepping closer, he places his hand on her cheek and whispers, "Of course, I was. Now, go change that shirt before we don't make it out of here at all." Liam gives her a wink. Shelby teases back saying, "Would that be so bad?" As she starts to make her way back inside, Liam sternly replies, "Shelby, don't tempt me."

Walking up and down the shoreline, the two find quite a collection of shells. "Look at this one!" Shelby yells jumping in the water grabbing a big, ridged conch shell before the waves wash it back out to sea. "You love this, don't you?" He asks. She replies, "What do you think? Callie and I used to spend hours out here when we were little. I can't tell you how many shells her poor mom had to throw out when she moved out of their house. Bags and bags of shells were hidden in her closet."

Laughing, Shelby looks out to the ocean thinking back to all the great memories Callie and she had on this very beach. Sensing Liam over her shoulder, she turns around to see him walking towards her with a sparkle in his eyes. The sun just peeking around him creates a silhouette of his body. Her nerves begin to take over as she mumbles softly to herself, "He is so tempting." Apparently, she mumbled louder than she thought, because he says with a smile, "Yes, you are." Mortified, she places her hands on her face and buries her head in them, embarrassed that he heard her.

Standing in front of her now he moves her hands from her face. "Shelby, you don't have to be embarrassed with me, ever. It's pretty clear the attraction we have for each other is pretty intense. If I said I was not standing here undressing you with my eyes, I would be lying. I told you last night, I'm trying to prove to you that I am good for you. If slow is what you want, then that's what you will get. If you just want to start out as friends and see where that goes, then I'll do that too," he says. "Obviously, we skipped the whole just friends part and went right to friends with benefits about a year ago," she says bluntly. Liam laughs under his breath and replies, "Fine if that's what you want then I guess I can do that too." Laughing loudly, she pushes him towards the waves. He snatches her up and carries her farther into the water. "Liam, don't! If you throw me in the water you will SO get it!" Laughing, he says, "Get what? I. Can't. Hear. You! What? What will I get, Shelby?" Liam lowers her body closer and closer to the water. "Liam!" She screams.

He pulls her back into his chest while cradling her in his arms, making their way back towards the beach, staring at her the whole way. She is filled with desire for him and it continues to grow deeper every time they are together. She likes this side of Liam, and also likes that they can enjoy each other and just have fun. Maybe she had been the one pushing him out this whole time, holding in so much anger for no reason. Maybe there really are no games and lies with him, just a nice guy. Just Liam.

Laying her back on the sand, he leans down on his side next to her. Shelby whispers, "Liam, thank you for bringing me here today. I am having a great time with you." Now relaxing and taking in the sea air, Shelby feels more in love than she has in a long time. Letting go, she lays down next to him and gently wraps her arms around his neck. "What are you thinking about?" He asks. "You," she replies. "And?" He questions. Smiling, but looking a little confused asks, "And what?" "Well, you can't say you are thinking about me and not follow it up with why." Shelby says in a snarky tone, "Yes, I can." Chuckling, he professes "Shelby, you drive me crazy. You drive me so crazy." He gently kisses her knowing he can't let her go again.

Chapter 9

"So, let me get this straight...you went on a date with Ted, Liam ruined that date, and you end the night by kissing Liam at the beach? Shelby!" Callie screams, with laughter. Annoyed, Shelby responds with narrowed eyes, "Ugh, this is why I wasn't even going to tell you. Plus, Ted and I just went out as friends, not a date! He's a sweet guy, and maybe if Liam wasn't in the picture, I would go out with him again." Callie interrupts, "Because you like Liam!" Rolling her eyes, Shelby replies loudly, "Yes, okay. Yes! Yes! I like Liam! There, I said it! Are you happy now?" Callie just smugly smiles at her.

About that time, Nate walks into the room mocking Shelby, "So, you do like him?" Shelby groans, "Ugh, why do you two gang up on me every time?" Ignoring her question, Nate interrogates Shelby even more, "So, anything else you want to say about Liam? Anything you just need to get out there?" Callie scowls at Nate. "Even if I did have something, why would I tell you?" Shelby asks crossing her arms. "What are you up to, Nate?" Callie questions. Laughing, he responds, "Oh, nothing, just that Liam is here in the other room and I was hoping I could get the scoop before he walks in." "Nate!" Callie yells. Standing up, Shelby punches Nate in the arm and heads for the kitchen.

Startled, Shelby stops abruptly, finding Liam sitting at the kitchen table kicked back, smiling at her. "How long have you been sitting there?" She questions. "Why?" Liam says with a teasing smile. Shrugging her shoulders and blushing, Shelby replies, "Just curious." She walks over to the sink to put her plate and cup from lunch in it. Just then, she feels Liam's strong arms around her waist, and he begins to softly kiss her neck. "Liam...not here," she mutters softly. "Why?" He whispers in her ear. "Because, I said so," Shelby demands, trying to move him off of her. Spinning her around to face him, Liam keeps his arms wrapped tightly around her while caging her in her against the kitchen counter.

Smiling, she places her hands on his chest as if she were trying to force him away. Standing there wrapped up in Liam Shelby finds herself completely hooked on this handsome, sexy man. With a smirk, he says, "So, you do like me, huh?" Rolling her eyes, she drops her head giggling and states, "You are such a pain." Laughing, he tilts her head up by the chin and looks directly in her eyes before saying, "I like you, too, Shelby. More than I think you know..." He kisses her softly. She twists her hands in the front of his shirt as he pulls her in close to his chest with one hand on her waist, and the other still locked in around her. She lets herself become lost in his words. Shelby thinks to herself how she doesn't want this moment to end. She doesn't ever want to let him go. The need she is beginning to have for him again is overwhelming.

"Could you two get a room?" Nate yells, annoyed. "Maybe they could if you would get this place finished!" Callie scolds. "Ouch!" Liam laughs, looking up to see Callie and Nate walking into the kitchen. Quickly, Shelby drops her head in an embarrassment of being caught. Laughing, Shelby wiggles out of his arms and heads for the door, Callie trailing right behind her. "Bye! We are headed to Sophie's shop. Nate, I'll be home later," Callie says, shooting Nate a smile. "Hey, Shelby!" Liam calls out. Halting at the door, she turns around to see what he wants, all eyes staring at her. "Will you have dinner with me tonight?" Liam asks nervously. Looking at Callie, then back to Liam, Shelby replies with a huge grin, "Yes, I would love to." Playing it cool, Liam says with a wink, "Great, see you at home, then." Shelby laughs at him and walks out the door, hearing Liam's laugh trailing behind her.

Hearing a knock at the door, Shelby looks up from the mirror realizing Liam is early. In fact, 20 minutes early. "Doesn't he know women are not always on time!" She gripes to herself as she heads for the door. "Hey, you are early," she says as she opens the front door, taking notice of how handsome he looks. Liam stood wearing dark fitted jeans with a light blue V-neck tee that showed off his muscular arms and chest. The things this man did to her, she thought. His hair was fixed, while his smile was smoldering.

Holding a bouquet of fresh sunflowers, he asks, "Do you want me to come back?" Smiling, she says, "No! Just come on in, grab a drink, and make yourself at home." He hands her the flowers and leans in to kiss her cheek. "Liam, you are too sweet. The flowers are absolutely beautiful!" She exclaims as she heads to place them in an empty vase on her dining room table. "I'm going to change, and then we can leave," Shelby says as she walks down the hallway to her room. Liam, confused, replies, "But, you are already dressed and look great, I might add!" Rolling her eyes, Shelby jokes, "Don't you know that women change their outfits at least three times before picking the perfect one out?" Laughing, he answers, "No, I must have missed that memo."

Closing the door behind him, Liam walks to the kitchen to grab a drink from the refrigerator before heading back towards the couch. Something caught his attention out of the corner of his eye. He stops in his tracks and lets his jaw drop, gazing down the hall. There, he sees Shelby standing in the bedroom doorway in a white, lace bra, black underwear, and red pumps. "Damn," he says to himself, gawking at her. Apparently, said a little too loud, because Shelby suddenly looks up and pushes the door shut. "Sorry! I was just getting up to get a drink and then I saw you standing there...WOW...," he trails off. "It's fine. I kind of forgot the hall leads to the front room," she responds with a giggle. "If you want to just stay in here tonight, we totally can!" Liam says casually. Laughing, Shelby teases, "You would like that too much, now, wouldn't you, Liam?" Answering honestly, he hollers, "Yes, I would!"

Standing there, he thinks to himself how perfect she is. Beautiful, smart, sexy, and full of sass. "Don't screw this up Liam," he coaches himself. He rubs his hands over his face, stunned at what he had just seen. Shelby is so fit; he's so attracted to her. After last summer, he had not been able to get her out of his mind. Taking a sip of his beer he continues to think about every curve of her body, her smile, and her laugh. Suddenly, Shelby makes her way into the room and he finds his thoughts interrupted. "Liam, I said are you ready?" Shelby says annoyed. Instantly, he stands up replying, "Yes, sorry I was just...thinking about something." Smirking, she says, "Well, let's go." Reaching out for her hand, Liam responds, "Shelby, I really didn't mean to stare earlier. I'm sorry, but you were just there and well, I honestly just couldn't stop looking. You are just so damn beautiful." Liam remains staring at her, lust filling his eyes. Shelby tilts her head to the side and leans up to gently kiss his cheek. "It's fine, nothing you haven't seen before, right?" She replies with a wink.

On the drive to the restaurant, Shelby can't help but think back to the last year. The night she thought she would never think of Liam the way she does now. She used to think he was someone she didn't want, but she may have been wrong. Completely wrong. And for once in her life, she was okay with being wrong. Hours later, they pull back up to their condo duplex. "I had a really nice time and dinner was so good, thank you, Liam," Shelby says as he turns off his truck. Walking around to the other side of the truck, he opens her door and helps her out. "I'm just glad you actually came with me!" He replies. "Did you think I would say no when you asked me?" She questions. "I honestly hoped not, but I didn't know. We have been so up and down lately and I didn't want to push you," Liam admits. "Well, I'm glad you asked me," she says smiling. "Let me walk you home," he says with a chuckle while motioning to the porch. Shelby laughs and jokes back, "Oh, thank you. A whole 10 feet!" Giggling, the two walk up to her front door. "Well, good night, Shelby," Liam says. "Good night, Liam," She repeats. The two just stand there staring at one another.

Liam drops his head down to hers and runs his hand through his hair. "God, you are stunning Shelby," he whispers to her. His words made her heart flutter and she leans up to gently kiss him on the lips. Memories begin to flood his mind of how this happened last summer. Shelby runs her hands through his hair, pulling herself in closer to his chest. Passion ignites between them, and they can barely contain their lust for one another. Hands begin to roam and the kisses turn harder. Pressing her back harder up against the wall, Shelby mumbles between kisses, "Liam." Pulling back, he begins to step away. Breathing heavy, he runs his hands through his hair again seeming frustrated at himself. He sighs, "I'm sorry, Shelby." Flushed, Shelby replies, "Liam, no, I kissed you." Laughing, he answers, "Damn, I love hearing that." Smirking, moving her shoulders up and down with each deep breath, her eyes locked on him.

Liam rubs the side of her face and says, "Shelby, I'm not going to lie to you. I want you, so bad. I have wanted you since the first time I saw you last summer. You are the only person I have been with since then, and all I can think about." As he said those words, he realizes how hurt he would feel if she says she had been with someone else. Luckily, she replies, "Same for me." Relief begins to settle in his mind. Stepping closer, he kisses her lips and makes his way to her cheek, but swiftly pulls away taking a few steps backward, just smiling at her. Shelby stands there frozen against the porch while watching him walk to his condo door. The connection between them is fierce. The farther she watches him walk away, the more her heart aches for him. Finally, as he opens his condo door, he looks to her one last time with a grin. Shelby smiles back with a wink and then spins around to walk inside her condo.

Chapter 10

Jumping out of bed, she rushes to her window to see if Liam's truck is outside. Frowning, she notices his truck is gone. She walks back to her room thinking of how quickly everything has changed. Later that afternoon, Shelby still hasn't heard from Liam. Callie and she was just leaving Sophie's shop when she notices Ted walking their way. "Hey ladies! How are you?" Ted asks. "Hey, Ted! I'm good, how are you?" Callie asks in return. "Well, I am much better now that I have been greeted with the two of you beauties," he replies. Callie blushes as Shelby rolls her eyes, jokingly replying, "Ted, you sure know how to make us girls feel good." Arrogantly, Ted replies with a wink at Shelby, "I sure do!" Callie's eyes grow wide as she stares at Shelby.

Walking towards Callie's car, Ted asks, "Hey, Shelby, can I chat with you for a minute?" Shelby answers, "Sure." Callie smiles and says, "I'm just going to put these bags in my car before we grab lunch." Ted goes on to ask Shelby, "So, I will be in town for a few more days and I was hoping you thought about my offer? Dinner tomorrow night?" Shelby sighs and says, "Ted, I had a really good time with you the other week...," but before she could finish, she looks across the street and locks eyes with Liam. His hard, dark stare glares back at her.

Liam is just standing there, staring at her, motionless. As their eyes connect, Ted looks to where Shelby's eyes wandered off to. "Okay, well, it looks like you are already taken then," he says in a mellow tone. Shelby looks back at Ted with a little guilt setting in and explains, "Well, I wasn't when we went out, but it just kind of happened right after that." Ted answers, "It's fine. I thought something was up at the wedding when he crashed our dance, but I hoped I still had a chance with you." Shelby apologetically says, "Ted, you deserve someone great. Any other time, I probably would have given you my full attention, but right now I can't." Leaning down, Ted kisses Shelby's cheek and smiles at her. "Thank you, Shelby," he mutters as he rubs her back and begins to walk away. Shelby quickly notices Liam walking across the street. Oh, boy, she thinks to herself.

Liam's fists clamp tight as he takes long strides towards them. Luckily, Ted made it back to his car before Liam approach Shelby. "What did he want?" Liam asks sharply. "Liam, relax. He was just saying hello," Shelby replies. "It looks like more than just hello to me," he snarks. Shelby rolling her eyes annoyed replies, "Actually, he asked me out, but I told him I was already taken." Liam's breathing begins to slow, and his expression weakened. "You did?" He questions. "Yes, I did. But, after I woke up this morning to find your truck gone and didn't hear from you all day, I thought maybe I had it all wrong," she says, awaiting his response. "Shelby, Nate called early and asked for my help. He's trying to surprise Callie by finishing the house today. He knows you two were going shopping, so I didn't want to tell you. I was going to call you later," he exclaims.

Putting her hands on her hips, she replies, "You should know I can keep a secret. Also, you should know that I didn't

like that I couldn't stare at you out my window this morning."
Smiling, he reaches for her and pulls her into his arms. Leaning
down, he eagerly kisses her. "Liam," she says looking around
to see if anyone is watching. "What? I want everyone to know
you are mine," He replies, laughing and dipping her on the side-
walk. "Yours? How did we determine that?" She questions with
a laugh, as he stands her back up. "Well, I would say it started
last summer," he jokes. "Not funny," she says shaking her head
and slapping his chest. Liam kisses her again with a smirk. "I'll
just be working for a few more hours and then I'll be home," he
responds winking at her. Giggling, she replies, "Well, then I better get you some dinner going, honey!" Rubbing her back while
wrapping his hands around her, he says, "I'll head over around
7 p.m." They kiss again, and as she watches him walk back to
his truck she feels her heartache at the loss of his touch.

Hours later, the two enjoy dinner together at Shelby's
condo. "Dinner was so good Shelby. I haven't had a home-
cooked meal in months," Liam praises. "Well, don't get used
to it," she jokes. He helps her clean up dinner and even offers
to do the dishes. Shelby sits on the counter drying the dishes
as Liam washes them. He asks her about her family, school,
and teaching. She counters by asking him about his past and
his family. "What do you think you will do after your job with
Nate is over?" Shelby asks. "Well, it's nice working for myself and consulting for bigger companies, but these smaller
deals that Nate has going here is really good. I like being in
one spot for longer periods of time," he answers. "You mean,
you like being here with me?" She questions. "That, too," he
replies with a grin. As Liam dries his hands off, Shelby asks,
"So, what about past relationships?" He pauses and inquires,
"What about them?" She questions further, "Did you have any
serious relationships?" Liam leans back against the sink and
explains, "I had a serious girlfriend in high school, but we both

went to different colleges. Long-distance just didn't work out. I have dated a few people since, but no one serious. What about you?" he probes. Shelby already knew this would come up.

"There was a guy in college I dated and we were pretty serious. We met there and dated for a year. He lived three hours from school and went home a lot on the weekends. I was never in a serious relationship before him and I thought he was the one. We talked about marriage and even looked at rings together, but one day he came over and told me he wanted to break up. He said that he was bored, and wanted to try something different. A few months later, I was at a party and ran into him and his girlfriend, who he had been dating for three years. I was heart-broken and promised myself I would never again get caught up in something like that." Tossing down the towel and looking at her with sadness, Liam replies, "What an ass! Shelby, I'm sorry you were treated like that." Shelby states, "It's fine. I was fine. I ate my tears away with Ben and Jerry's ice cream for about a month and then began running. Running helps me clear my mind."

Liam steps towards Shelby and wraps his arms around her. Shelby places her hands on his shoulders, then wraps her legs around his back. "Shelby, I would never ever hurt you, you know that, don't you?" Liam questions. Shelby, hesitating, replies, "Yes, I do. I know now." Softly, he admits, "Shelby, you are amazing and perfect. Do you know that, too?" Shelby sighs, shaking her head replying, "No, I am not. Far from perfect." Liam demands, "Yes, you are!" Shelby leans in to gently kiss him on his lips. Liam starts to move his hands from her back up to her neck and lightly presses his body to hers, cupping her chin with one hand. Shelby digs her fingers into his shoulders, wrapping one arm around his neck pulling him even closer to her.

As they begin to kiss one another softly, in a matter of seconds their lips become fully emblazoned. Liam places his hands around her back reaching to pull her legs tighter around him, picking her up off of the counter. Walking towards the couch, still intensely kissing, he lays her down flat. Never breaking their kiss, Liam positions himself on top of Shelby on the couch, propping himself up by his forearms. "Liam," Shelby mutters breathlessly in his ear. "Shelby, I can't help myself, I want you so badly. God, I have missed you," he says panting between breaths.

She pulls at the back of his shirt, wanting to rip it off of him. Liam rapidly yanks his shirt off and throws it to the floor. Shelby admires the man above her, instantly thinking how caught up in him she is. "Damn, I missed this," Shelby exclaims. Liam smirking, begins to press deeper into her lips, and asks, "Like what you see?" Now blushing, Shelby answers, "You already know I do." His hands begin to slide up her shirt, pulling it off, and roam across her bare skin, taking every inch of her body in. His hands rub softly across her lace bra causing her pulse to quicken as her thighs pressed tightly together. Overtaken by desire Shelby moans his name and then lightly whispers in his ear, "Liam, can we go to your room?" Barely able to catch his breath between their exchange of passionate kisses, questions, "What?" Assertive now, Shelby says, "I want to go to your room," Liam looks up to her, thinking he knows exactly what she wants.

He scoops her up, leaving his shirt on the floor, and carries her out her front door to his condo. Both glad their condos are set back in a private drive. Shelby snickers as they walk down the porch, "Good thing the Charleston's are out of town!" Laughing, Liam replies, "Good thing! They wouldn't get any sleep tonight with all the noise we are about to make." Shelby lays her head on his shoulder gently brushing her lips down the side of his neck. Liam can feel her hot breaths on his neck and shoulder, his thoughts anxious with want and need. Turning the knob and kicking his door open, he places her down ŏn the couch, and then quickly spins around to close his door. Shelby sits there breathing heavily, looking around nervously, thinking back to the last time she was here. Liam walks over to pick Shelby back up as she giggles and carries her down the hall to his bedroom, where they shared their first special moment together last summer.

The two stare into each others' eyes, never breaking their gaze. Shelby's eyes now filled with lust and an overwhelming feeling of just being in this moment with Liam. She leans her head down to his. Gently turning her face back up with his fingers, he looks to her and asks, "What do you want, baby?" She smiles as she remembers him saying those words to her last summer. "You know exactly what I want, Liam," she boasts with a smirky grin. The two let passion take control. They vigorously undress each other, letting clothes flood onto the floor. The two begin shuffling amongst the sheets completely naked, picking right up again where they left off last summer. They explore each other's bodies', making new memories they will never forget, and becoming lost in one another again.

The sun is barely peeking through the curtains as Liam opens his eyes, finding Shelby curled up in his arms. Liam begins to smile to himself, thinking back to last night, knowing it was exactly what he has wanted for so long. He thinks to himself, now he has her and she is going to stay his forever this time. Lowering his lips to her back, he begins to kiss between her shoulder blades while pushing the sheet down lower on her body, admiring her perfectly toned figure. "Liam, why are you up so early?" Shelby grumbles. Smiling, as he continues to plant kisses up her spine, he replies, "Because, I can't sleep with your naked body lying next to me." Shelby continues to mutter, "It is so early. What are you doing?" With her hand over her mouth, laughing, she says, "Sorry, morning breath!" Liam chuckles, replying, "Morning breath and all, I wouldn't change a thing about this very moment. Shelby, I could wake up like this every morning." Shelby blushes as Liam leans over to kiss her.

Looking around, she notices the room is bare. "Liam, where are your things at?" Liam rolls over to his back staring up at the ceiling and groaning, replies, "I'm not sleeping in here anymore. I took the other bedroom." The confusion begins to settle on Shelby's face. "Why? This room is much bigger and it has the attached bathroom," she says. "Yes, it is, but it also has memories I couldn't bear to relive when I first arrived back here," he explains, now appearing a little embarrassed at what he just admitted. Shelby's brows lift in surprise as she questions, "You mean, us?" Taking a deep breath in and sighing, he replies, "Yes." He buries his face in his hands in embarrassment and continues to explain, "It was too hard to think about what happened last summer when I first arrived back to the condo. Plus, having you a few doors down just made it that much worse." Shelby, smiling at the sweet gesture, leans over to him and crawls on top of him kissing his exposed chest. "Then, I guess we'll have to make new memories, won't we?" She says as she tries to tickle him. Smirking, he pulls her up towards his face and replies, "Yes, we will!"

Chapter 11

Later that afternoon Callie and Shelby layout on the beach soaking up the warm sun rays and enjoying the cool, light breeze that was blowing on them. "Callie, I'm so jealous that you will get to do this whenever you want!" Shelby says. Callie smiling, responds, "You could, too, you know?" Shelby rolls her eyes and says, "Oh really?" Callie explains, "Yes. The new school is opening up next year and they are still looking to hire several more teachers. The pay is great, and the beach view isn't too bad either!" Callie laughs. Shelby thinks to herself what it would be like to move here and live next to her best friend. "What am I going to do, be the third wheel to you and Nate forever?" Shelby questions laughing. "No, looks like you have found something much better to keep yourself entertained," Callie says motioning towards Liam, as he and Nate walk towards them on the beach. Shelby glances back at Callie with a smile and demands, "It's not like that, Cal!" Callie replies sarcastically, "Okay, keep telling yourself that, Shelby!"

The two men approach the girls carrying a cooler, while Liam tosses a volleyball into the air. "You ladies ready for a little competition?" Nate asks them. "Oh, you know we are!" Callie says accepting the challenge. Liam, looking directly at Shelby, says, "Hey there!" Quickly, Liams drops to his knees in front of Shelby to give her a kiss. The two just sit there staring at each other, as if no one else is around. "You mind if I barge in on your girl time today? I can't really handle being away from you, and let's be honest, that bikini isn't helping anything," Liam admits. Shelby giggles and slaps his chest playfully, then whispers to him, "I can take it off if it would help." Liam grins in surprise at her frisky comment. Shelby sees the tint of fire igniting in his eyes.

"Okay!" Nate says loudly, pulling Liam up away from Shelby. "No fraternizing with the enemy Liam. We are here to teach these two how to play some volleyball. Ladies, come on!" Nate goes on to say. Callie laughs as Nate smacks her on the ass. Shelby passes Liam and ever so lightly brushes against his shoulder in a flirtatious manner. "You ready for this?" Shelby asks smiling. "Absolutely. You two are going down!" Liam responds. Liam pulls his shirt off and tosses it to the side of the volleyball net. Shelby moans lightly in awe of his body, "Oh, Jesus." Callie laughing, asks, "So, do you disagree about the whole finding 'something better' comment now?" Shelby smirks and replies looking at Liam's now bare chest, "Not at all."

As Nate hits the last volley over the net, Shelby begins running back to hit it. She jumps high into the air and crashes to the ground, completely missing the ball. She laughs at herself, thinking about how silly she probably looked. Instantly, Liam dips his body under the net, running over to help her back up. Nate swiftly scoops Callie up into his arms and begins walking them towards their beach chairs.

Shelby grabs the volleyball and Liam pulls her up by her hands. "Looks like we win," Liam says with a smirk. Shelby begins dusting the sand off of her body, rolling her eyes, and responds, "We'll see who wins next time!" The two turn around and head for their beach chairs when suddenly Shelby spots a familiar face heading towards them on the beach. Freezing in place, she drops the ball. "Shelby, everything okay?" Liam asks her. Blinking her eyes, she answers, "Yes, everything is fine." As Liam glances up he sees a man walking towards them.

"Shelby, I thought that was you. How are you?" The man says as he leans in for a hug. Liam's body tenses as he watches the guy hug Shelby's barely clothed body in just her bikini. "Hi, I'm great. How are you doing?" Shelby replies nervously. The mysterious man answers, "Doing good. I just got back into town a few days ago. Gosh, I haven't seen you in forever! I saw Sophie a few days ago and she told me you were here, so I was hoping I would run into you." The man begins to look up at Liam, sticks his hand out in a kindly gesture, and says, "Hey, man, how's it going? I'm Tyler." Wanting to be polite, Liam meets Tyler's handshake and simply says, "Hey." Shelby jumps in, "Sorry, yes, Tyler, this is Liam. He's a friend of mine. Liam, Tyler and I were, well..." Tyler interrupts, "Friends! From way back." Tyler now smiling at Shelby. Walking up behind them, Callie's shouts, "Holy crap! Look what the cat drug in!" Callie laughs as she meets Tyler for a hug. Nate follows closely behind her, shooting Liam a look.

"I'm in town working on a proposal for the new nature preserve. I work for the state agricultural and animal program. We just got a new grant for this area and since I grew up here, they thought it would be best to design the updates. I'll be here for another week or two finishing up the project. I would love to take you all out to dinner and catch up," Tyler says. Callie smiles and responds, "Wow, that is awesome! You sure were always so good at that stuff." Tyler further explains, "Well, I love animals and the sea, so here I am. After this as-

signment, I'm looking to move back to Tennessee." Liam realizing that is the same place that Callie and Shelby are from
looks to Shelby with an inquisitive face. Tyler continues saying, "Yeah, it's been so much travel lately. I'm just ready to
finally settle down." Tyler looks directly at Shelby with a gen-
tle smile. Shelby quickly diverts her eyes away from Tyler and
changes the subject. "That's great. Yeah, maybe we can all try
to meet up. Well, we were just leaving, so we will see you soon
hopefully, Tyler," Shelby says. "Yeah, I better catch up to my
colleagues. We took the day off to enjoy the sun. Do you still
have the same number, Shelby?" Tyler asks. "Yep, same one."
Shelby answers. "Great, I'll call you soon. Nice to meet you all,"
Tyler says as he turns around and walks back down the beach.

Shelby turns around and starts walking back to the beach
chairs. Liam following closely behind her. "So, want to tell me
who he was?" Liam asks. Callie and Nate swiftly follow behind the two of them. "Yeah, Cal, who was Mr. Smiles?" Nate
jokingly asks. Callie rolls her eyes at Nate and answers, "He
was just a childhood friend. Tyler's parents had two houses,
one here and one in Tennessee. His parents traveled a lot with
their jobs, so he was never really in one place. The summers
we would see him here and we all always hung out. We left for
college and occasionally would still try to meet up. I haven't
seen him in a few years." Shelby staying quiet looks up to Callie. Nate asks, "Okay, so what's the story then? He was smiling
way too much to just be a friend. Callie, I'm not mad, just curious. Did you and he have a thing?" Liam looks at Shelby with
worry. Shelby sighs, taking in a deep breath, looks up to all of
them, and says, "No, they did not." Callie interjects, "Shelby."
Shelby goes on to say, "No, it's fine. Tyler and I, well, we used
to hang out. When he would come to Nashville he would stay
with me." Liam's eyes grow wide to this news. "So, you were
friends with benefits?" Nate questions laughing. Callie shoots

her daggering eyes at Nate. Nate realizing what he just said, responds, "I'm sorry, Shelby. I didn't mean to say that." Looking directly at Liam, Shelby replies, "No, it's fine. He was thereafter my college boyfriend broke up with me. It's all old history. Not a big deal."

Liam starts to put his shirt back on and begins to collect the cooler and volleyball he brought. "I think I'm going to head out," Liam announces. "Liam!" Callie shouts. "Come on, man, how about we kick their butts in one more game?" Nate teases. "That's okay. I'll pass on this one," Liam replies tossing Nate the volleyball. Turning around he begins to head towards the parking lot. "Liam!" Shelby yells. Putting her hands to her face she shakes her head in frustration. Liam is so jealous right now, Shelby thinks to herself. Callie frowns at Shelby. "Sorry, Shelby, I didn't mean to rub it in on him. I really wasn't thinking when I said that." Nate says over Callie's shoulder. "No, you weren't," Callie scolds. Shelby grabs her bag and swim pullover as she runs up the beach towards the parking lot.

When she reaches Liam's truck, she finds him just sitting there. She asks, "Liam, what are you doing? Why did you just walk away from me? Tyler is just a friend...was just a friend." Shelby opens the truck door and hops inside. Liam looks at her and says, "I'm sorry, I just can't stand the thought of you being with someone else." Shelby responds, "It was a long time ago and well before us." Irritated, Liam rebuttals, "Us? So, now there is an us? Is there really even an *us*?" Sternly Shelby responds, "What! I thought there was after last night?" Shelby now looks to Liam with defeat in her eyes. Heavily sighing, Liam answers, "I don't know. I feel like as soon as we get something good going, then another hurdle jumps in our way. You introduced me as a *friend*, Shelby. What should I be thinking? First, our past gets in the way, then Ted, and now

Tyler?" Loudly, she hollers, "You are just so jealous!" Perplexed, he questions, "Jealous? I'm not jealous, but damn, Shelby. It seems like every guy we run into wants you or has been with you." As soon as the words left his mouth his eyes grow wide and he mutters, "That's not what I meant." Gasping, and now annoyed, Shelby screams, "You are such a jerk, Liam!" Opening the passenger truck door, Shelby jumps out as Liam shouts her name, "Shelby!"

Liam enraged, punches his fist into the steering wheel. He sits there thinking about how he ruined their day together. He looks over and sees Nate and Callie pulling out of the parking lot without Shelby. Frantically, he starts looking around and can't find her. Stepping out of his truck he begins to look around the parking lot. Walking fast towards the beach where they had been, he looks out onto the sand. Turning back around, he sees Shelby out of the corner of his eye getting into a silver SUV. As he gets closer, he sees it is Tyler who she is with. The two drive off. "You have got to be kidding me!" He shouts out loud to himself. Quickly rushing over to his truck, he jumps in and puts it into drive.

Tyler and Shelby pull into her condo driveway. "Tyler, thank you for bringing me home," Shelby says smiling. "I'm just sorry if I caused any issues with you and your boyfriend, Shelbs," Tyler apologizes. "You didn't, and he's not my boyfriend," she replies. "He's not?" He questions. "No, he is not. Just a friend," she explains. "By the glances, I was getting from him and his clenched fists when I gave you a hug, I for sure thought I was going to get my butt kicked," he says laughing. Sadness now filling her eyes, she responds as she steps out of the SUV, "I'm really sorry, Tyler." Closing the door and leaning down through the passenger window she continues to say, "It's just complicated right now." Looking at her across the vehicle, he says, "Well, you deserve the best!"

Hearing the roaring of his tires as he comes to a sudden halt, parking his truck in front of Shelby's condo. He quickly jumps out of his truck, as the dust settles, and shouts, "Shelby! What are you doing?" Liam begins to walk towards her. Shelby exclaims, "I got a ride home from a friend, Liam. You sure as hell weren't giving me one!" Tyler looks at Shelby and says, "I'm going to go unless you need me to stay?" Now raising his voice, Liam intervenes, "No, she doesn't need you to stay!" Shelby sneers, "Don't speak to him like that, Liam!" Tyler tensing his fists on his steering wheel says, "Shelby, I don't think you should stay here. Why don't you get back in the car?" Liam approaching Tyler's SUV snarls, "What did you say?" Shelby yells, "Liam!" Opening the door, Tyler repeats, "I think Shelby realized who she really needed when she got in my vehicle, bud." Shelby yells, "Tyler!" As soon as she rounds the vehicle she sees Liam punch Tyler square in the mouth. "Liam!" She screams.

Just as Tyler hits the ground, Nate's truck pulls into view. Tyler jumps up and tackles Liam. Although Liam is better built than him, Tyler is quick and gets a jab into Liam's left side. Liam gasps as he doubles over. Tackling Tyler to the ground, the two roll around with Shelby screaming at them both. Nate jumps down and pulls Liam back. "What the hell is going on here," Nate asks. Their fists are still flying and the two are now covered in dirt. Liam spits the dirt out of his mouth while Tyler wipes blood from his. Shelby screeches, "Liam, what are you doing?" Liam looking confused yells at her, "Really, Shelby? Come on!" He responds. "You get in his vehicle and have him drive you back home while I have to watch it all, and then ask me what the hell I'm doing. So, last night meant nothing then?" Shelby's eyes begin to fill with tears. Tyler looking to Shelby as he walks to his SUV, says, "I'm leaving!" Shelby shouts as she runs toward him, "Tyler, wait! Please come in and let me help you get cleaned up." Liam drops his head and shakes it as he moves out of Nate's hold. "You good?" Nate asks. "I am just great," Liam sarcastically responds as he walks to his condo.

"Shelby, come here. What is going on? What was all that talk about Liam at the beach, and now you are walking into your condo with Tyler?" Callie asks. "It's not like that. I caused all of this, so the least I can do is get him cleaned up. I'll let him wash up, give him ice, and then I'll talk to Liam." Shelby explains. Callie puts her hand on her friend's shoulder and frowning, says, "Shelby, you need to figure out what you want from Liam. I love you, but you are killing his heart." Shelby's brow raises up in shock and questions, "Whose side are you on, Callie?" Callie assures, "Yours, of course. But this is not okay." With a frown, Shelby agrees, "I know, Cal. I'm really sorry." Callie runs to meet Nate who is walking towards Liam's condo, leaving Shelby and Tyler at her front door.

While Shelby stands in her kitchen, she sees Callie and Nate drive away. "Thanks again for letting me clean up, Shelby," Tyler shouts from the bathroom. "It's the least I can do. And again, I'm so sorry I got you into my mess." Shelby yells back. "It's fine, but it seems like I'm good at getting into trouble with you," he laughs. Tyler was there as a friend for Shelby after her college boyfriend broke her heart. He took her out to parties to try to make her ex-boyfriend jealous. One thing leads to the next, and finally, they had taken their jealousy plan to a whole new level. Shelby and Tyler began seeing each other more frequently, on a *friend with benefits* kind of level.

Tyler walks out of the bathroom brushing his blonde, wavy locks with his hand. Shelby compares the two men in her mind; Liam is sexy in a rugged, hardworking, and muscular kind of way, but Tyler is tall and thin, toned, and more sophisticated looking. Tyler has always been the fun guy that she loved to hang out with, but he is definitely flirtatious with everyone. She thought once about him as boyfriend material but was never too serious about it.

Tyler walks up to Shelby as she stands in the kitchen and says, "Well, I'm going to go." She replies, "Okay." He moves closer and leans down to kiss her cheek. "Shelbs, call me if you need anything. And if you decide to ditch your crazy neighbor, give me a call okay," he jokes with a smirk. As soon as Tyler makes it to his vehicle, Shelby throws herself on her bed and begins to cry. Shelby sits on her bed thinking about what she should do. She knows she needs to talk to Liam, but she also knows what she did was coldhearted. She didn't think it all through. When she stormed off from Liam at the beach and he didn't immediately follow her, she ran into Tyler who was also leaving. He asked if she needed a ride and she accepted. She didn't realize Liam got out and chased after her. When she saw him pull into the driveway, she knew there was going to be trouble.

Tears streaming down her face as she walks to the bathroom. She begins to disrobe and steps into the shower. Standing directly under the showerhead, she lets the hot water run down her face. She places her hands on her face and begins to sob, thinking about how she royally messed things up with Liam.

Chapter 12

The next morning, Shelby walks out of her room intending on apologizing to Liam, but when she opens the door, she notices his truck is gone. A sense of guilt rolls through her emotions and the sudden need to just be with him pulls at her. Countered with both culpibility and disgust Shelby thinks back to the expression Liam held for her in the change of events yesterday. His sadness rolled off so easily, but his words hurt. Looking around, she figures he must be helping Nate with a job. She sends a text message to Callie.

Sorry about yesterday. Liam makes me crazy. By the way, is he helping Nate today?

Shelby's phone lights up. It's Callie calling her. As soon as Shelby hears Callie say the words, she drops the phone...he left.

Still talking on the phone, Callie explains, "Liam told Nate he had an emergency pop up with a job a few towns over that he had to handle and would be back in a few days. Shelby, I'm so sorry." Shelby holds her tears back, replying, "It's fine. I should have known this would happen. We are good at hurting each other and then leaving." Callie sighs, "Sweetie, maybe you two just need some time apart, and then you can try again." Saddened, Shelby replies, "Callie, two people should not have to try and try to make something work. It should just happen." Callie speaks softly, "Love is tough, Shelby." Shelby interjects, "Love! We are not in love!" Callie laughing, replies, "Okay, friend, whatever you say. Anyways, Nate and I have a dinner party to attend tonight. Do you want to tag along?" Shelby politely declines, "No thanks, I'll be fine on my own tonight. You two enjoy your evening together."

Hours and a few pints of Ben and Jerry's ice cream later, Shelby falls asleep. She wakes up to a knock at the door. Blinking away her sleepy eyes, she looks at her phone. It reads a quarter til 10:00 p.m. Blinking again, she gets up and walks to the window to look out into the dark night. She sees a man, but can't tell much more. Hesitating, she asks, "Who is it?" The man answers, "Liam." Shocked and angry, Shelby pulls the door open quickly and yells, "Why did you leave?" Sarcastically, he responds, "Hello to you, too." Shelby puts her hands on her hips annoyed and snarls, "You left me, Liam. You just left!" Looking down to the ground, he replies, "I had something come up." Cutting him off, she calls, "Bullshit, Liam! That's the easy way out." Shelby tries to push the door close, but he catches it before it slams shut. Shelby groans, "Go home, Liam!"

Liam pushes his way through the door insisting, "No, Shelby, I won't." Shelby steps back trying to hold in her anger. "You really think I'm not sorry about what happened?" He asks with sorrow. He continues to explain, "I'm not sorry about punching that dude in the mouth, but I am sorry about getting so jealous and causing a scene." Shelby closes her eyes and puts her face in her hands. Looking back up, she says, "Liam, I'm not mad at all about the fight. I caused the fight, I know that. I'm mad because you left me. You didn't even talk to me, you just left. Lastly, on top of that, the other night was perfect with you, and then you left me just like that." Tears fill her eyes and begin to drip down her cheeks. "Shelby," he mutters stepping closer. "I had to. I was so angry and hurt. I just needed some space and time to think. Shelby, you had your ex drive you home while I had to follow behind in my truck. Plus, you couldn't even tell him we were together." Pausing and listening to his words, she begins to cry even harder.

Liam begins to run his hands through his hair. Walking towards her he pulls her into his arms. "Please, stop crying, Shelby," he begs as he rubs her back. Whimpering and wiping her tears away, she wiggles out of his arms. Calming her breathing and wiping even more tears away, she says, "This is what we do, Liam. We fight. We argue. We are not good for each other." He feels his gut-churning as he hears those words, thinking they all sound too familiar. Shelby continues, "I just can't, Liam." His body tenses at her words and he realizes what he has to do. Before she could finish, he steps back and says, "You are right, Shelby. You really are right this time." Walking out of the front door, he looks back and says, "I really am sorry for everything. Enjoy the rest of your summer Shelby." When the door closes, she falls to the floor sobbing. Gasping for air, she sits on the floor clutching her chest and buries her head in her knees. It hurts so bad she thinks to herself. Red-faced from crying, she saunters to her bedroom with her heart in a million pieces.

Chapter 13

The next few days went by leaving only two weeks left of summer break. Liam stayed at the condo but avoided Shelby at all costs. Any time Shelby saw Liam she kept her head down so he wouldn't see her tears, but it didn't even matter because he always walked the other way. She destroyed any chance they had together, and she regrets that now.

"Shelby, just be honest and tell him how you feel," Callie instructs. "It's too, late," Shelby replies. "It's never too late, look at Nate and me. We have been through so much together, and look we finally made it. It's quite the love story if you ask me," Callie voices as she reaches for Shelby's hand. Callie further explains, "Shelby, I know you have always been a planner, but sometimes things don't always work out the way you want them to. You two are good for each other, but I think you have been so afraid to let him in that you keep pushing and pushing him away. Sweetie, he's a good guy and I think he loves you, Shelby, I really do. Nate said he's been miserable these last few days, just like you are. You just have to let him in. Not everyone is like your ex." Shelby smiles at Callie and says, "Thanks, Cal." She's thankful for the love and support Callie shows her, but finds herself lost in the poor decisions she has made with Liam.

On her way home from lunch, Shelby thinks about what Callie said. They always get so close, and then she finds herself pushing Liam away. Love is scary, and the last time she let herself love someone, he lied and broke her heart. But, Liam is different. He hasn't done much wrong, well, other than punching Tyler, but she caused that drama to happen.

Pulling up to the condo, she sees Liam sitting on the porch fixing a tool. "Hey," she says as she walks up to him on the steps. "Hey," he mutters, shyly looking up at her. He looks so sad; it hurts to see him like this. "What happened?" Shelby asks, looking at the tool on his lap. "I was helping Ruby today on a new condo she bought, and my blade on this saw slipped off track. I'm just trying to fix it, so I don't have to shell out four hundred dollars to buy a new one." Liam explains. "It didn't hurt you, did it?" She questions with sincere worry etched on her face. Looking up, he grins and replies, "No, it didn't." Liam refuses to give Shelby his full attention.

The two linger on the porch trying to engage in awkward conversation to avoid the tension in the air. "Wow, those are expensive for how small they are," she says about the tool. He looks back up and laughs agreeing, "Yes, they are. How have you been?" Now looking at her anxiously. "I have been good, I was just out to lunch with Callie," she replies. "Oh, girl time," he says with a smirk. Shelby thinks about that smirk, oh, how she has missed that so very much. Just seeing him sitting there, she wants to wrap her arms around him and kiss him all over. She wants him so bad. Thinking of all the times they bickered back and forth, and even then, deep down she knew she still wanted him. Regardless of everything they have been through, she just wants to be wrapped up in Liam's arms.

Smiling at her, he asks softly, "Shelby, what are you thinking about?" With a slight smile, she answers, "Nothing. I was just thinking about a few weeks ago when you were trying to fix the bathroom sink." He chuckles and replies, "Yeah, and you thought you could do it better than me. How did that turn out again?" Shelby smiles and laughs, letting out a snort. "Did you just snort?" He asks, bursting out in laughter. Shelby covers her mouth, embarrassed by the noise she just made but continues reminiscing on that day. Shelby remembers telling him what he was doing wrong with the sink, not considering this is what he does for a living. When he tried to do it her way, the pipe to the sink busted. Liam fixed it his way angrily and quickly as they bickered in the bathroom. In the midst of their heated argument, the two just stopped, looked at one another, and suddenly found themselves wrapped in each others' arms, lost in their passionate affection.

Standing up and then stepping down closer to her, he says, "Well, I better get back over there." Stepping back and looking up at him, she asks, "Where to?" He explains, "The new condo over on Edgewater that Ruby bought. I'm almost done with the shutters and I'd like to finish them up today before the big storm comes." Shelby questions, "Storm?" Liam goes on to explain, "Yeah, we are supposed to get some pretty big storms heading our way. They could kick north, but they aren't sure yet. I'd rather play it safe." She replies, "Yes, of course." She hesitates before saying, "Okay, well, please be careful." Pausing, he smiles at her, and says, "I will. Have a good night Shelby." They both just stand there for a minute as if they had more to say. The two look at each other, lingering, before Shelby breaks the silence, replying, "Good night, Liam." She turns and walks back to her condo. Before she walks in, she looks back over her shoulder and sees him walking to his truck. For a brief moment, she thinks about running to him and telling him all the things she wishes she had already said. However, she knows the hurt she caused him and deep down thinks it is best to finally let him go.

Liam is right, the storms are rolling in, and the rain has already started. Shelby sits watching the weather and keeps a lookout for Liam's truck. He hasn't finished at Ruby's yet unless he went somewhere else afterward. That thought makes her sick to her stomach; Liam possibly out on another date. The rain is pouring outside and the wind begins to howl as the storm moves in closer. Palm trees are swaying back and forth, while the sand and brush swirl across the yard. A loud noise begins to bang outback, so Shelby runs to the back-bedroom window to peek out. Looking out, she sees a piece of the top of the gazebo had fallen off and was swinging back and forth hitting against the side of Ruby's greenhouse. Thinking to herself, she knows she needs to get that big piece of wood down or it could break the side glass to the greenhouse.

Throwing on a coat and her flip flops, she pulls her front door open, but suddenly a gust of wind slams it open into the wall inside her condo. She grabs it and pulls hard, fighting against the wind and rain. She finally closes it behind her as she stands outside. Looking down the long porch, still not seeing Liam's truck, she thinks that maybe she should wait for him to see if he could help her, but she didn't know if he was coming back home or not. Looking out to the sky, she sees large, dark clouds heading their way, as the storm sirens seem to get louder in the distance. She takes a deep breath and runs out into the storm.

Chapter 14

As soon as Liam saw the storm radar on the diner TV, he knew he needed to get back to the condo. He jumps in the truck and starts listening to the weather on the radio, trying to beat the storm home. Pulling back up to the condo, Liam turns off his truck. Severe weather with hurricane-like winds were heading right for them. Nate calls to tell Liam he is heading back to check on Shelby. Walking up to the condo, his heart stops and his fists clench when he notices Shelby's condo door standing wide open, swinging back and forth. It had taken him almost 20 minutes longer to get home than normal due to the strong winds and pouring rain.

Running to her door, he rushes inside yelling her name, "Shelby! Shelby!" He runs to each of the bedrooms, but still can't find her. His heart is racing as adrenaline rushes throughout his body. Lightning strikes, making a loud roar. The condo windows shake, causing Liam's panic to fully set in. "Shelby, baby, where are you?" He whispers to himself with worry. Running back outside, he screams her name again, "Shelby!" Running around back, he looks towards the greenhouse...nothing. The wind picks up and pushes against him as he tries to make his way back where the gazebo sits. Wiping his face, he tries to clear the rain from his eyes. The wind is howling and wet sand is stirring up through the air. The lightning lights up the sky, and the trees sway back and forth. Another lightning bolt strikes the ground and Liams shouts in extreme fear, "Shelby!" Looking farther away on the backside of the gazebo, he sees something on the ground. As he moves closer, his heart stops.

"Shelby! Oh my God, Shelby! Baby!" He screams as he runs to her and drops on his knees to the ground. Shelby is laying on the ground with her face buried in the wet dirt and sand. Covered in muddy water, she groans, "Liam." Liam frantically says, "Baby, I'm here. Shelby, oh my God. What happened?" Her voice weak, she groans again, "Liam." Barely touching her, he asks, "Are you hurt? Where does it hurt?" She tries to move her arm to touch her head, but she moans in pain. Lightly moving her head to the side, he sees blood. His eyes grow wide and full of fear. The wind knocks a huge pile of brush right into them, knocking Liam over. Sitting back up, he covers her from another pile heading their way. "Shelby, can you move, baby?" Mumbling, she tries to speak, "Yes, I think a little, but my head, Liam. It hit my head," she says. Looking around, he sees a huge piece of wood laying nearby. "Shelby, I've got you. Can you hold on to me?" Before he raises her up from the ground, he checks her arms and legs to be sure everything else is okay.

Picking her up, he cradles her into his arms as the wind is fully blowing against them. Liam heads back towards the front of the condo with Shelby in his arms. "Hang on baby," he tells her. Gripping her tightly, he pushes through the forceful wind as the rain pelts him in the face. Shielding her face with his, he tucks her closer into his chest. As he rounds the front of the condo, the wind suddenly swipes him, knocking him down to his knees. Off-balance, he tries to catch himself from falling and dropping Shelby. Cradling her to him as he fell to the ground, he rolls on his back with her elbow jolting his jaw. "Ahh!" He groans. "Liam," she whimpers. "Shelby, I'm sorry, I have you, I'm so sorry." Standing back up, he walks a few more steps towards the condo, watching one of Ruby's wind chimes blow away off of the corner of the house. Walking up the steps, he kicks open his door, walking inside with Shelby still cradled in his arms.

Inside, Liam sits Shelby down on the couch gently. He rushes back to her once he closes the door, and pulls her hood down off of her head. "Shelby," he whispers with sorrow in his voice. She opens her eyes as he wipes her face off, blood dripping down everywhere. Liam sees a gash on the left side of her face and asks worried, "Shelby, what were you doing? Grimacing, she tries to sit up, but struggles. "Shelby, I think you have a concussion, and you may need stitches on your head. We need to get you checked out, but we shouldn't go out until the storm passes," he explains. Shelby closes her eyes, tears filling the corners. Liam leans in front of her and grazes his hand over her cheek. Her voice soft and shaky manages to say, "I was so scared. I just wanted you, Liam." Liam leans in closer to her and promises, "I'm here, Shelby. I'm here now. I'm not going anywhere." He kisses her hand, and then her cheek.

Liam wraps Shelby in two big blankets, and finds a washcloth to clean her head with; he holds pressure on her cut to stop the bleeding. Once the blood dries up, the gash doesn't seem nearly as big as he had originally thought. The blood made it look much worse. Granted, it was still terrible that this happened to her. Callie and Nate had been calling both Shelby and Liam. When neither answered, Nate was about to head over to their condos to check on them when Liam luckily catches him on the phone before he makes his way out in the storm.

"Dude, you wouldn't answer. We were so worried," Nate explains to Liam. Liam tells him the story of what happened and assures him that as soon as the storm passes he is going to take Shelby to the Emergency Room. Callie, of course, is not happy with that answer. Nor is she happy about being away from Shelby, knowing her condition. However, with the storm still covering the beach, there isn't much she can do right now. "At least you are there with her, Liam. That makes me feel better," Callie says, reassuring herself. Liam feels comfort in that statement from Callie and replies, "Thanks, Callie." He set a timer to go off every hour to check on Shelby in case he accidentally falls asleep.

At one point through the night, the storm began to settle and he kneels on the floor, next to her watching her sleep. Shelby is still sitting on the couch, wrapped up in blankets. As Liam places his hand on her chest, feeling her heartbeat, he whispers in her ear, "Shelby, I'm so sorry, baby. I'm just so sorry this happened to you." Wiping a tear from his face, he thinks about the hurt that he caused both of them. He caused Shelby's physical and emotional pain. Liam on the other hand is mentally and emotionally pained. He rarely cries; his tears represent full of pure pain and anger. The minute he saw her lying there on the ground, not moving, he prayed that she was alright. He would do anything to trade her places. He just wanted her safe. That moment, Liam knew he would never leave her again. He loves Shelby; he loves her with his entire being. He loved her with his entire soul and nothing will ever change that.

Hours later, Liam wakes up blinded by the sunlight coming through the window. Looking up, he notices he fell asleep knelt next to Shelby, holding her hand. Glancing up to her face, he sees her eyes staring wide open at him. Her beautiful, soft eyes. "Hey," she says, still not moving her hand from his. Liam sits upright holding her hand tight and replies, "Hey, how are you feeling this morning?" Shelby goes on to say, "I'm doing okay. My face is still very sore, and I have a huge headache. I went out to try to fix the gazebo, I saw a piece of wood dangling from the top in the middle of the storm. When I reached for the piece of wood, the wind caught it and slammed it back into me, knocking me to the ground unconscious. I am not sure how long I was out there, but I remember being very cold and wet." Tears now streaming down her face, she tries to keep her composure. "I was so scared, Liam," she says sobbing now. "Baby," he mutters as he leans up closer to gently kiss her cheek, trying to comfort and calm her down.

Liam moves onto the couch beside her. She cuddles up next to him and lays her head on his chest as he wraps his arms around her, bringing them closer to one another. She looks at the dried blood on his shirt and asks, "What happened there?" As Liam replays the story out loud, Shelby stares at him in horror. "Shelby, I was so scared when I saw you there, just lying on the ground, not moving." He puts a hand to his face and runs it through his hair in pure agony at the events that took place last night. "Shelby, I just don't know what I would do if I lost...," his words cut off by a knock at the door. Callie shouts, "Shelby! Shelby! Liam, open this door now!" Liam looks at Shelby smiling, and says, "Are you ready for the rest of the storm?" Shelby laughing, replies, "I guess let her in."

After an hour of bickering with Callie, Shelby gives in. She lets them take her to the Emergency Room. Nate drives them while Liam stays behind to clean the place up. A tree fell in the back by the gazebo where he had found Shelby. The greenhouse had no broken windows, but the door is completely blown off. One of the wood posts on the porch is cracked from a chair striking it, and Ruby's windchime is unsalvage-able, shattered in the driveway. As Liam stands there looking around, he suddenly thinks about Shelby and what would have happened if he had not come back last night. There was no doubt in his mind that he was going to return, but he needed to disappear for a few days to cool off. He was stricken with anger and jealously. Now realizing his ego got the best of him and Shelby was right, he couldn't fathom losing her. He almost lost her for good this time. Standing there, with his hands to his face, full of guilt, he thinks about all the pain he has caused her.

Nate's truck pulls back up outside Liam's condo. Liam sitting on the front porch jumps up to rush to Shelby as soon as he sees her. Shelby looks terrible; she has a huge white bandage on the left side of her face and purple bruising surrounding her eyes. "Well, what did they say? Are you okay?" Liam asks. "I am doing okay, just a little tired. That's all," she replies. Nate hands Liam the discharge papers as he helps Callie get Shelby inside. "The doctor said she had a mild concussion, the gash on her face needed five stitches, and the doctor said to take it easy the next couple of days. He said no driving and no running, just relaxing," Callie instructs. Shelby rolls her eyes, taking a deep breath in and insists, "I am fine." Liam demands, "No, you are not fine, Shelby. You are going to do what the doctor said and just relax." He lays the papers on the table, turns around, and continues saying, "I will take care of you. I am right next door. I will help you with whatever you need. I'm always here for you, Shelby." Shelby looks up and responds, "Liam, you don't have to do that." Stepping closer, he says, "Shelby, I want to and I need to." The two stare at one another in silence. Their lust for each other evident they long for one another in that moment.

Callie and Nate stare at each other in disbelief. Nate touches Callie on the arm and says, "We will come back tomorrow." Hesitating, Callie shoots Nate an annoyed look but doesn't fight him because she knows they should go so Shelby can rest. Shelby looks up at Liam and exclaims, "Really, I am fine. I can take care of myself!" Liam glares at her and says, "You may be able to take care of yourself, but I am not going to let you do that on your own. I am here, Shelby. I want to be here for you."

Callie kisses Shelby on the head and makes sure she has food and a drink beside her. Getting a blanket, Callie covers Shelby up on the couch. Callie says her goodbyes before she and Nate walk out the front door. Liam sits next to Shelby on the couch, and when he goes to speak Shelby cuts him off and insists, "We need to talk." He replies, "Okay, I think we need to talk, too, Shelby." Shelby turns her body towards Liam, grasps his hands, and explains, "I know that we have been through so much craziness since last summer. I know I haven't been easy on you at times, and I made our relationship even harder than it needed to be, or at least the relationship we tried to have ..." Liam tries to interrupt her. "Let me finish," she demands. "Okay, sorry," he answers softly, nervously rubbing his hands on his knees. "Liam, I used to wish that we had never met, but through all of this, I think I have figured out that I am thankful to have met someone like you. I admit I do have feelings for you, and if we weren't in our current situation then maybe our relationship could work. However, we live hours and miles apart from each other. We are just two different people that allowed our feelings and summer fun to get the best of us, clouding our better judgment. Love isn't meant to be this difficult, but it also isn't supposed to be as easy as a summer fling. I can't give up everything I have worked so hard for. I simply won't," she explains with a sigh, tears beginning to fill the corners of her eyes.

Listening to Shelby, Liam's chest is pounding and his heart is breaking. Thoughts of hurt, anger, and confusion all swirl through his mind. For the first time since he met her, he really didn't know what to say. He knows that if he lets his temper show, he might say something he will regret later. He knows what he wants, and he knows she is wrong about their relationship. He thinks they are perfect for each other, as crazy as it may seem, she is his world. Liam decides in that second that he needs to let her figure out her feelings on her own.

Shelby stares at him waiting for his response. He responds softly, "Okay. Whatever you want, Shelby. I just want you to be happy." Shelby stunned by his response, lets her eyes fill with even more tears now. Liam begins to get up from the couch. "That's it? That's all you have to say?" She asks. "What do you want me to say?" He asks genuinely. "Not that," she replies. He looks to her with confusion. "Shelby, I told you, I just want you to be happy. If that's how you feel, like we shouldn't be together, then I guess that's it for us." She stands up and heads for the door. "Shelby!" he shouts behind her, lunging for her arm as she reaches for the front door. With tears on her face, she turns around to hear Liam say, "Let me help you today, please. Shelby, you still need someone to help you after last night." As she motions further out the front door, she says, "I do, but just not you, Liam." Shocked, Liam sits back on the couch thinking *this is it*. He knows he has to let her go, even if it isn't what he really wants.

Chapter 15

Liam and Nate sit at the diner in town. Nate is scolding Liam for how stupid both him and Shelby had been. "Come on, Liam, don't you know you have to fight for things sometimes?" Nate exclaims. Liam shoots him a glare and responds, "I tried man, it backfired." Rolling his eyes, Nate laughs and says, "Shelby loves you, man, and she's stubborn as hell. Don't give her a choice." Liam laughing out loud, responds, "Easier said than done, and are we talking about the same woman?" Liam asks. Just then, the doorbells ring as Callie and Shelby walk through the front door of the diner.

Shelby's face fills with worry, as she spots the two men in a booth near the back door. Liam glances up and shoots Nate a look of frustration. "Really?" He asks sarcastically. Liam immediately stands up and walks out of the back door. Shelby blinks back tears as she stands there watching him leave. Why was she upset? She asks herself. He doesn't want her anymore, and it is all her fault. She ruined everything. Her stomach drops and heart races. Callie's voice breaks the silence by saying, "I'm sorry, Shelby. Nate and I were just trying to help." As Nate approaches them, Shelby pushes past him heading for the back door, determination in each step.

Just as Liam steps in his truck and sticks the key in the ignition, he spots Shelby standing in the parking lot staring at him. Her beautiful gaze catches his eyes and he stops just before putting the truck in drive. His heart feels heavy and his hands grip the steering wheel as he watches her stand there, shoulders moving up and down and tears in her eyes. Shelby bolts out in a sprint to his truck. Pushing all the hurt aside and allowing his true feelings for Shelby to the surface, he throws off his seatbelt and swings open his truck door, jumping out to meet Shelby. She swiftly leaps up into his arms. Their lips intertwine and arms wrap around one another as if they had never missed a beat. Never breaking their kiss, Liam holds on to her tightly and spins her around pressing her against the truck. Cars honk their horns in approval as they pass the love scene taking place outside the diner.

Shelby blushes with embarrassment. "Hi," she whispers pulling back from him. "Hey," he replies with a smirk. "I'm so sorry, Liam. I was scared and filled with so much emotion..." Liam interrupts, "Shelby, I love you." He softly cups her face with one hand as the other still wrapped around her, holding her up. With raised eyebrows, she looks up to his eyes, astonished at what he just said to her. "What?" She asks. Lowering her on to her own two feet, Liam repeats, "Shelby, I don't care if this is all crazy, or if we are both too stubborn to understand each other sometimes. I know that I am deeply in love with you and it hurts even thinking I can't have you for the rest of our lives. It kills me to not wake up with you or to see your beautiful face every day." A huge smile appears on her face as she pulls his head down pressing their lips together. Softly, she says, "I love you, too, Liam, so much." Grinning from ear to ear, he lifts her up into his arms holding her with an abundant amount of love, allowing their lips to become fully emblazoned.

Realizing he is moving them, giggling she asks, "Liam, where are you going?" Barely removing his mouth from hers, he opens the passenger door, places her in the seat, and says with a wink, "Home." A combination of giddiness and lust runs through her body as he closes the truck door. The desire for him at this moment far exceeds her confused emotions. Leaning his arm on the window smiling, he says, "We are going home to make up instead of giving the entire town a show right here in this parking lot." Blushing, she puts her face in her hands and laughs as he pulls them back down giving her one last kiss. Running around the truck, Liam jumps in and begins to pull out of the parking lot as Nate and Callie stand at the diner door with blank stares. "Don't come by for a few days, we have plans!" Liam yells out the window winking. Smirking, he waves goodbye as Shelby shakes her head and wrinkles her nose in embarrassment. Laughing, Callie and Nate hug each other and then give one another a high five as Liam and Shelby drive away.

Chapter 16

2 years later....

"The breeze never gets old," Shelby says as she looks out the window with Callie next to her. "No, it sure doesn't," Callie says, laying her head back and closing her eyes, letting the breeze catch her hair. Smiling at one another, Callie asks Shelby, "Are you ready?" Shelby lets out a big sigh, "Yes! I am soo ready," she says with a huge smile. "Wait! How are you feeling?" Shelby asks Callie while looking down at her round belly. "Well, considering I am seven months pregnant and you are making me wear this dress while standing outside in the blazing heat, I am just perfect," Callie replies sarcastically. Laughing, the two smile at one another as they walk out the back door.

Rounding the corner, Callie and Shelby stand outside of Liam and Shelby's new home that Nate and Liam had just finished remodeling a few months ago. Both couples are living at the beach near each other and they couldn't be any happier. Liam moved to Orange Beach and partnered with Nate's construction company, allowing the two men to take on more commercial bids and corporate designs. Their business is booming, only getting busier and busier. Shelby found a teaching job here as a 5th-grade science teacher and Callie continued to tutor kids. Callie loves the one-on-one time teaching the children, plus with the pregnancy it allows her to be able to manage her schedule much easier. Walking out the door to the beach, Shelby feels the sun beaming down and a slight breeze flowing through the air. Taking a deep breath, she closes her eyes for a moment to take in the salty air, smell the fresh cut flowers, and remember all of the love that was shared on this very beach. Smiling to herself, she looks towards the water and sees Liam standing there staring right at her.

His smile is so contagious. Her heart is full, realizing he would soon be with her forever. Nate stands next to Liam, as he is his best man. Shelby snickers to herself when she sees the worried look on Nate's face. She knows Nate is scared that Callie's water might break right here on the beach. Callie and Nate took no time getting pregnant, announcing the pregnancy soon after they got married. They had a sweet and simple beach wedding last year. Seeing her best friend so unbelievably happy brought her so much joy.

Walking down the aisle towards Liam, Shelby feels butterflies in her stomach. Taking her hand from her father's, Liam leans in to give her a soft kiss on the cheek. The two stand there holding each other with more love than they ever could have expected. The pastor asks if they are ready to begin the ceremony, drawing everyone's' attention to the bride and groom. The pastor motions for everyone to stand as they exchange their vows. As the pastor announces them as husband and wife, the crowd cheers them on as they exchange their first married kiss. Chuckling, Liam looks right at Shelby and whispers, "I love you so much." Shelby smiles back at him and repeats, "I love you, too, Liam." The two walk down the aisle, hand in hand, as the new Mr. and Mrs. Brooks.

Author's Note

THE END

I hope Love is a Storm brought you as much joy as Love on Shore, if not more! The second book was definitely my favorite, as the lives of all the characters unfolded. Learning many things from the first book, I took note and adjusted for the second, hoping not only for a better read, but also to melt the hearts of all my readers. The journey through these two stories has helped me reflect back to some good and bad times throughout my own life. Knowing the end result with my own love story, it reassures me that I would do it all over again.

More info

For more information about upcoming books from this Author be sure to check out, ajohnsonpublishing.com.

Find her on Instagram @author.ajohnson.

9 781087 897950